Murder
Lost and Found

Debbie Young

Copyright Information

About the Author

Debbie Young writes warm, witty, feel-good fiction, inspired by her daily life in the beautiful English Cotswolds.

Her Sophie Sayers Village Mystery series follows the life of the fictitious village of Wendlebury Barrow from one summer to the next, and her Staffroom at St Bride's series will run the course of a school year. She also writes short novellas in the same setting under the series title Tales from Wendlebury Barrow.

Her humorous short stories are available in themed collections, such as *Marry in Haste*, *Quick Change* and *Stocking Fillers*, and in many anthologies.

She is a frequent speaker at literature festivals and writers' events, is founder and director of the free Hawkesbury Upton Literature Festival.

A regular contributor to two local community magazines, the award-winning *Tetbury Advertiser* and the *Hawkesbury Parish News*, she has published four collections of her columns offering insight into her own life in a small Cotswold village where she lives with her Scottish husband and their teenage daughter.

For the latest information about Debbie's
books and events, visit her Writing Life website,
where you may also like to join her free Readers' Club:
www.authordebbieyoung.com

Also by Debbie Young

Sophie Sayers Village Mysteries
Best Murder in Show (1)
Trick or Murder? (2)
Murder in the Manger (3)
Murder by the Book (4)
Springtime for Murder (5)
Murder Your Darlings (6)
A Fling with Murder (8) – coming soon

Staffroom at St Bride's Series
Secrets at St Bride's (1)
Stranger at St Bride's (2)
Scandal at St Bride's (3) – coming soon

Short Story Collections
Marry in Haste
Quick Change
Stocking Fillers

Essay Collections
All Part of the Charm
Still Charmed
Young By Name
Still Young By Name

To school administrators everywhere
May your lost property cupboards always be empty

"Eyewitnesses who point their finger at innocent defendants are not liars, for they genuinely believe in the truth of their testimony. That's the frightening part – the truly horrifying idea that what we think we know, what we believe with all our hearts, is not necessarily the truth."

Elizabeth Loftus, writing in Psychology Today

"It never does you any good to compare yourself to others. No matter how bright or capable or athletic you are, there will always be someone smarter or slicker or faster."

Kate Blake

Murder
Lost and Found

© T E Shepherd

HAWKESBURY
— PRESS —

1 Deal

"As going out of my comfort zone to Greece made such a difference to me, I think it's your turn now."

In May, a week's writing retreat on a tiny Greek island had inspired me to start on my first book, *Best Murder in Show*, recording some of the many notable episodes in my life since I'd inherited my great-aunt's cottage in the Cotswolds.

On the first day of the school summer holidays, with no school-run mums to serve in the tearoom, I was taking the opportunity of a quiet moment in the bookshop to thrash out an important subject. After nearly a year of dating, Hector and I had yet to take our first holiday together.

Hector raised his eyebrows.

"Why? I'm pretty well-travelled. I've been around."

"Yes, but not lately. Ever since I've lived in Wendlebury Barrow, you've never been further than Clevedon to see your parents. Aren't you getting a bit set in your ways for a man of thirty-two?"

He tapped on his music app to change the tunes playing over the sound system. Then, to the mellow tones of Ella Fitzgerald singing Gershwin's "Summertime", he strolled over from the trade counter to sit at a table in the tearoom.

"I hope you're not thinking of a trip to Australia to see Horace? That's way beyond my budget just now."

Appealing as visiting Hector's identical twin might be, that wasn't what I had in mind.

"No. My idea would be much cheaper. Let me show you Scotland. You've never been there, and my parents would put us up for free. They live in a lovely part of Inverness, right on the river, just up from Ness Islands. It's a great base for exploring the Highlands."

Hector folded his arms in resistance, but I knew the way to his heart.

"Inverness has a huge second-hand bookshop. A booklover's Aladdin's cave."

He uncrossed his arms.

"Maybe. But not until the end of the school summer holidays. So many local parents rely on us to liven up their children's long vacation. Besides, I can't afford to be away from the shop during peak tourist season."

We'd already started our summer holiday activities programme for children, as the colouring sheets and craft materials on the play table suggested.

"OK, deal. Which reminds me, I promised to go and help rationalise the school library today."

"I thought you did that on Friday?"

"No, that was only a quick check, and I could see at a glance I'd need more time to do a proper job. Can you spare me for an hour or so this afternoon?"

"If you think you can stand the excitement."

I set a coffee in his favourite mug on the table in front of him. Ella Berry, the school's highly efficient business manager, is one of my best friends in the village, and I'm always glad of the excuse to visit her, but I wasn't going just for fun.

"The school's latest book order arrived this morning, so I thought I'd take that up and get it out of the way in our stockroom. Besides, it'll give me an opportunity to identify any gaps in the library stock and give Ella ideas on how to spend next year's book budget. Ordering from us, obviously."

Hector always says I'm good at spotting opportunities to grow his business.

"OK, Sophie, that's fine. A summer afternoon in the village school library – what could possibly go wrong?"

2 Lost Property

The school entrance hall looked just the same as in term-time: staff headshot photos arrayed in a neat grid on the noticeboard, glass-fronted case full of trophies, wooden board displaying the names of each year's head boy and head girl, lost property spilling out of the understairs cupboard beside the office door.

But in the school holidays, the smell was distinctly different. Gone was the invisible fug of school dinners. If I were a perfumier bottling its essence, I'd say thick base notes of floor polish cut through by astringent heart notes of disinfectant, finished with refreshing top notes of new-mown grass. On my way to work that morning, I'd heard the putt-putt of the mower making its first full cut of the school holidays.

With the children now despatched, I'd expected to walk into silence. No strident voices of teachers in lessons, no cheery buzz of high-pitched chatter at playtime and lunchbreak, silenced at key moments by the tolling of the old-fashioned handbell. Yet the school was awash with noise, emanating from behind Ella's door.

I knocked much harder than usual to announce my arrival. Even though I've been entrusted with the entry code for the front door, I never feel I can just barge into Ella's office, whether on an errand from Hector's House or a social call after work to lure her up the High Street for an early evening drink and supper at The Bluebird.

Above the blaring beat, I could just hear footsteps in time with the music – footsteps, possibly dancing. I wondered whether anyone else was in there with her: the headteacher, or one of the teachers. Most people assume schools close down during the holidays, but, as a former teacher myself, I know a skeleton staff is on duty all year round.

My arms were aching now beneath the weight of the box of new stock, and I needed to set it down. The heatwave that had obligingly started with the school holiday was making me far warmer than was comfortable, even in the loose Indian cotton dress that I'd found in my late great-aunt's wardrobe. When after my second knock, I heard no invitation to enter, I assumed Ella's music was drowning out all other sounds, so I pushed the door with my elbow.

"Anybody home?" I shouted as the door slowly swung open, startling Ella who was striding about the room. Her cheeks rosy from exertion, she crossed to her desk to mute her Bluetooth speaker, before flopping down into the chair behind her desk. I set the box of books on her meeting table and flexed my arms in relief.

"Sorry, Sophie, I didn't hear realise you were here." She gave a nervous giggle as she reached for the on button of the coffee machine. "I wasn't expecting you just yet. I thought we said you'd sort out the library this afternoon?"

I settled back in her comfortable visitor's chair, glad she was going to make us coffee.

"I know, but it's all quiet in the tearoom, so I thought I might as well deliver your latest order to get the box out of the way in our stockroom. I hope I'm not putting you out?"

When she waved a hand dismissively, I guessed I was putting her out, but that she didn't like to say so. She dropped a coffee pod into the top of the machine, filled a mug for me, then repeated the process for herself. The mugs bore the logos of rival photocopier brands. As I added milk from the jug on her desk, she tapped the top of her Bluetooth speaker.

"There have to be compensations for being left in sole charge of the school the minute term ends."

"Sole charge? Are you the only person on duty? Isn't Mrs Broom here?"

Mrs Broom is the headteacher.

"Well, Ian's here, but he doesn't count." Ian is the school caretaker, a kindly middle-aged man I'd met through the Wendlebury Players, the village drama group. "Mrs Broom and all the teaching staff pushed off for their summer holidays as fast as felons jumping bail. They won't be in till mid-August at the earliest. I'd never be allowed to play my music if Mrs Broom were here. Although it's quite a musical school, its recorder band just isn't my vibe."

From the pocket of my dress, I produced a small package and peeled back the foil wrapping to reveal two sturdy fingers of shortbread topped with caramel and chocolate.

"Well, here's one of the compensations for my job: free millionaire's shortbread. It's left over from Saturday, so I can't sell it in the tearoom today, even though it's perfectly edible."

"Shouldn't it be called billionaire's shortbread these days?" Ella seemed unusually reticent to take a piece. "According to the romance novels I read, every eligible man and his dog is a millionaire these days. Millionaires just aren't rich enough to be of any interest."

I wrinkled my nose. "Hector isn't even a millionaire."

"And he doesn't have a dog, either, although that would be easier to remedy than his wealth deficit. Still, if you will hook up with a humble shopkeeper, what do you expect? You want to shop around a little more."

I took a sip of my coffee. It wasn't as nice as the coffee I make at Hector's House, but I was glad to be waited on for once.

"I didn't realise how much of a dog person Hector was until I got a cat." This issue worried me far more than his financial status. Just before Easter, Billy Thompson, one of our regular tearoom customers, had persuaded me to adopt Blossom, my coal-black kitten, from an eccentric old lady with a surfeit of cats.

"You two live too much in each other's pockets, that's your trouble."

In my heart, I wondered whether Ella was right. Maybe that was one reason Hector had been so keen to get me out of the way for a week without him in Greece. Unbeknown to me, he'd entered me into the competition that had won me the free place on the writers' retreat. Nearly a year into our relationship, we hadn't moved in together, even though we are each lucky enough to have our own place big enough to share. We had never even discussed whose place we would live in if we did: his flat over the bookshop or my cottage.

I wasn't ready to discuss all that with Ella, so I steered her back on track.

"Anyway, would it be OK for me to sort your school library out this morning rather than this afternoon?"

I glanced at the wall clock over the mantlepiece. The open fire remained as evidence of the school's origins in Victorian times, when education first became mandatory. This had once been the resident teacher's sitting room, and the fireplace came in handy when Ella needed to burn confidential papers.

"To be honest, this afternoon would be better. I haven't emptied the lost property cupboard yet, and I know I'll find a ton of library books in there, and goodness knows what else. On Friday, the last day of term, one girl even found her little brother in there when she was looking for her lost pencil case. He'd crept away from the leavers' assembly, unnoticed by his mother who was weeping as the top class sang their traditional goodbye song. There's no point touching the library until I've dug those out. Honestly, why the kids can't return their books to the library beats me, when it's only a few steps down the corridor. But frankly, it hasn't been front of mind this morning. I've had more important things to worry about."

"Like what?"

She picked up her pen to tap the neat list of points in her page-a-day diary.

"The contractors have just arrived to install the new playground equipment, then later this week I'll have to contend with the deep cleaning company's annual visit, and the drain men. Plus I've got until Friday to finish the end-of-term accounts."

I extracted a tissue from the box on her desk to wipe my hands before touching any books.

"The drain men? They sound sinister, like some villainous race from *Dr Who*. One false move and they'll suck out your soul."

"Or in our case, the septic tank." Ella licked melted chocolate from her fingertips. "The school's sewage system is finally moving into the twenty-first century. We're having our outlet pipes connected to the mains drainage system beneath the High Street."

"You don't have mains drainage?"

She shook her head. "Nor did anyone in Wendlebury until after the war. Anyway, I won't be able to get to the lost property cupboard until after lunch. Sorry you've had a wasted journey."

Her mind already on her next task, she got up from her desk to fetch a thick manilla folder from a shelf. "You wouldn't believe the amount of paperwork that went into getting permission for the sewage connection. Honestly, you'd think mains drainage would be a basic human right in a first-world country, not something you have to make a case for."

She extracted a folded sheet of paper of the kind architects use for building plans to show me the footprint of the school site. A red dotted line ran from the playing field behind the school, through the playground, under the security gate at the side of the building and across the forecourt to the High Street.

"Apologies in advance for the noise the contractors will make. Their pneumatic drills set my teeth on edge – another reason I brought my speaker in this week, so as to drown out that horrible sound."

She'd kept her office window shut to ensure she didn't share her music with half the High Street, even though it made the room stuffy. For the last few days, all sounds had travelled extra far in the thick, still, humid air. At least, if she turned her music off, she could use her sash window for ventilation. In the shop, the only opening window is a small one beside the front door, next to the trade counter. The main display window is fixed closed. It wasn't as bad for Hector, sitting at the trade counter, but in the tearoom at the back of the shop, where I spend most of my time, it was particularly muggy.

Ha-ha, muggy, I thought, a good tearoom pun. I stored it away to use on Hector later.

I folded the empty foil that had contained the shortbread into a flat square and slipped it into my pocket to recycle later. Leaving Ella studying the site plan, I left her office and was about to head for the front door when the mess spilling out of the lost property cupboard caught my eye. As Hector wasn't expecting me back yet, I decided to do Ella a good turn and save her some work by fishing out the library books buried among the debris.

I'm always happy to help out with the school library as all its new stock comes from Hector's House. Not all the local schools are such good customers. Hutmarton a couple of miles away hasn't bought a single book from us in the year I've been working at the shop, nor will the head let us streamline their library stock for them. My guess is that they fear the shelves looking empty next time school inspectors visit. Even so, it's hard to justify keeping books like *A Child's Guide to Amstrad Computing* unless they plan to use it in a history lesson.

As the music began to blare again from Ella's office, I threw open the double doors of the lost property cupboard and switched on the interior light. It was worse in there than I'd expected. I took a deep breath, then regretted it, inhaling odours of discarded sports kits and ancient packed lunches.

Stepping back from the overpowering aroma, I stumbled against a warm, sturdy mass that hadn't been there a minute before. With a shriek, I swung round, only to find Ian grinning at me.

I've known Ian for nearly as long as I've known Ella, first encountering him at the previous summer's Village Show. He was cast as the executioner on the Wendlebury Players' carnival float, which took as its theme Henry VIII and His Six Wives. Although Ian's sinister appearance had made small children cry as the floats processed down the High Street, we all knew that beneath his mask he was really a gentle giant, the much-loved lollipop man – the old-fashioned phrase still used in the village for school crossing supervisor. I'd tried to redress the balance by casting him as Joseph in the Nativity Play I'd written for the village community the previous Christmas.

Ian had recently added the responsibilities of caretaker to his employment at the school, swapping his high-visibility jacket and hat at the start of lesson-time for the less conspicuous brown duster coat: the school caretaker's traditional camouflage.

"Don't tell me Ella's roped you into emptying the lost property cupboard? She was hinting earlier that I might do it."

"Actually, she doesn't know I'm doing it. I just thought I'd give her a nice surprise, as she seems a bit stressed right now."

"Well, don't let me stop you. Just leave anything in usable condition on the floor and I'll take it to the charity shop in Slate Green when I get a moment. I'll fetch the bins round from the back of the school so you can easily get rid of any rubbish. The one for general waste is by the front door already – I must have forgotten to return it after the bin men came on Friday. I'll bring the ones for paper, cardboard and textiles round too as you're bound to need them."

He pulled a pair of rubber gloves out of his pocket and handed them to me. "You might be glad of these. I happened to have them on me, ready for my next task, but I think you'll need them more than I will. Besides, I can get another pair. I've a boxful in my cleaning cupboard. I always like to have plenty of spares. I've got three of these duster coats, too." He patted his lapel.

Grateful, I slipped the rubber gloves onto my hands, scissoring my fingers together to push them on fully.

"So, what are you up to next, Ian?"

"Cleaning the boys' bogs. Sorry, I mean toilets. That's what the kids call them. Toilet humour, eh? They never seem to grow out of it, not at primary school, anyway. Best of luck with the lost property cupboard, Sophie. With any luck, you'll find a treat or two that will make it all worthwhile. Last summer, I found an unopened box of Maltesers only a month past its sell-by date, and very nice they were, too."

"Thanks," I said flatly, as he turned to march down the corridor.

I gazed at the muddle before me, wondering where to begin. Then, as if playing a game of jackstraws, I went for the easy wins first. The top layer seemed to be mostly clothes, while heavier objects such as books and backpacks had sunk to the bottom of the heap, the arrangement reminding me of the different strata of geological deposits. It was hard to believe that so many clothes could have been lost without some of the children going home in a state of undress.

I extracted a pair of pillar-box-red Wellington boots that lay either side of the central mound and stood them neatly on the hall floor beside the cupboard. Next, I spotted a pair of tiny black daps, those old-fashioned slip-on gym shoes that I remember wearing as a child myself. Sticking out of the bottom of the pile was a much larger trainer – some of this year's leavers were almost the size of adults. So far, I couldn't see its pair, but I reckoned it had to be in there somewhere, because who loses just one shoe without noticing?

I pulled the trainer out, then sifted through the pile for its twin, which I found under a yellowing white school polo shirt. When I tried to tug it free, it slipped from my grasp. I leaned into the cupboard to loosen it from whatever was trapping it, perhaps the strap of a backpack or the tangles of a skipping rope. It seemed to pull back, as if instigating a Sports Day tug of war.

When I gripped it harder, I realised there was something stuck inside it. Impatient now, with my free hand, I swept all the clothes on top of it to one side. What I revealed made me reel, and I steadied myself on the door frame.

"Ian," I yelled at the top of my voice. Ella had paused her music, presumably to take a phone call, so I didn't want to interrupt her. "Do you think the charity shop will accept a dead body? Because I've just found one."

3 Lost Life

Ian didn't respond. Half-afraid the dead body might leap up and chase after me like a zombie, I slammed the cupboard doors closed and darted back to Ella's office. I swung the door open, this time without knocking.

Seated at her desk, she gasped in surprise, hurriedly wiping her eyes with the back of her hand.

"Sophie, I thought you'd gone. Whatever's the matter?" Her cheeks were damp and flushed with alarm.

"You'll never believe what I've just found in the lost property cupboard." I beckoned her to follow me. "Come and see for yourself. Brace yourself for a shock, though."

She folded her arms across her chest, not stirring from her chair.

"Lost property cupboard? What are you doing in my lost property cupboard? You're not meant to be snooping about in there. You're only meant to be tidying the library."

Talk about ungrateful!

"Is that the thanks I get for trying to do you a good turn? As you seemed so overloaded, I was going to sort it out for you as a favour, while also rescuing any library books. But that doesn't matter right now. I've got something much more important to tell you." I took a deep breath. "I've found a dead body in the lost property cupboard, hidden beneath all the junk in there. It was just lying there, as if it was asleep, but when I reached out to touch one of its hands, poking from beneath a navy hoodie, it was as cold as a gravestone. Come with me, I'll show you."

Ella leapt up from her chair and came out from behind her desk to join me. As we left her office, I linked my arm through hers, as much for my benefit as hers. We approached the cupboard slowly, putting off our chilling encounter. Then, just as I'd summoned all my courage to open the doors, Ella's arm slipped from mine, followed by the rest of her, as she slithered down into a heap on the floor.

I bent down to check she was still breathing, and once I was sure she was, I shifted her head into a more comfortable position. Then I sprinted to the boys' toilets. Not the most obvious first aid tactic, but I was hoping to find Ian there. As the green cross on his staff photo indicates, Ian is a trained first aider.

As I approached the boys' toilets, I could hear him cheerily singing "My Favourite Things". A couple of years ago, the Wendlebury Players staged *The Sound of Music*. When I reached him, I almost threw my arms around him with relief, but drew back when I remembered what he was doing.

"Ian, come quickly, please, and help me. I've just found a dead body."

The gentle smile that had lit up his face on my arrival vanished as he laid down his toilet brush and bottle of bleach.

"What is it, a mouse? A rat? A frog? Don't tell me Miss Wilton forgot to take the school hamster home. Poor little thing. If I were the head, I wouldn't allow classroom pets."

I shook my head. "No, it's not that little. It's nearly as big as you."

Ian's brow furrowed.

"Whereabouts?"

My mouth was so dry I could hardly get the words out.

"Lost property cupboard."

"*Lead on, Macduff,*" he said, then added conversationally, "Of course, that's a popular misquote. What Shakespeare's line actually says is, *Lay on, Macduff.*"

Trying not to mentally cast Ian as the murderous Macbeth and Ella as his wife, I trotted behind him as he strode masterfully up the corridor to the entrance hall. As dramatic as any character from a Shakespearean tragedy, Ian fell to his knees beside my still prone friend.

"Oh no, not my lovely Ella!" His cry rebounded down the empty corridor.

"*She should have died hereafter.*" Macbeth's words played in my head as if I were a prompt in the wings – although I would have been a pretty poor prompt, as that line is from a completely different scene to the one Ian quoted. Then Ian's misunderstanding shook me out of my stupor.

"No, no, Ian, Ella's not the dead body. She's just fainted."

"Oh, thank goodness for that!"

Just then, Ella's lips parted, and she let out the lightest of breaths.

"Air, she needs air," declared Ian. "It's stifling in here."

As easily as if she were one of the pupils, Ian scooped Ella up in his arms, cradling her head in the crook of one

16

elbow, her knees in the other, and strode towards the double doors that led from the corridor to the playground.

"Open the French doors onto the playground for me please, Sophie. The code's Agincourt."

"But there aren't any letters on the keypad."

"The date, 1415. The Battle of Agincourt. Mrs Broom's a history buff."

"Oh, I see! I thought it was just a coincidence that the code for the main entrance was the Battle of Bannockburn."

I punched in the code, held the door open for him to pass through, then followed him out onto the tarmac, slightly soft beneath the brilliant sunshine. I could feel the heat of the gleaming dark surface through the thin soles of my sandals.

When he reached the edge of the playing field, Ian laid Ella gently on the freshly mown grass to a chorus of wolf whistles from the trio of workmen who were clearing the site for the new playground equipment. They downed tools to come over to see what we were up to.

"You brought us a little present, boyo? How very kind."

The tallest of them nudged the speaker in the ribs.

"Hush now, Dai, there's ladies present."

"Yes, but only one of them can hear us," replied Dai, winking at me.

As Ian began to check Ella's vital signs, I stepped between the workmen and my friend.

"How can you be so insensitive, you buffoons? Can't you see she's not well?"

Two of them lowered their eyes and shuffled their feet, but Dai flashed a white-toothed smile at me.

"Sorry, lovely, just my bit of fun. I expect this heat is too much for her, eh? She wants to try slaving out here in the full sun, like what we are. Let me show you my top tip for keeping cool." He began to unbutton his shirt. "Just in case you're short of ideas."

I averted my eyes as he slipped his shirt off and chucked it on the grass.

"Now, Dai, behave yourself," murmured one of his mates. "You don't want any more trouble like last time."

"OK, back to work, you lot," piped up a familiar clear voice behind me. "We're paying you by the job, not by the hour, so no point stringing it out."

I don't know what Ian had done to bring Ella round, but she had made a remarkable recovery. It was hard to fathom how someone could go so quickly from unconscious to vigilant.

Joking among themselves, the workmen picked up their tools and got back to work. I knelt beside Ella, who was now sitting up, leaning back on her arms, legs stretched out in front of her.

"My goodness, Ella, you gave me a fright." I tried to sound cheerful to put her at her ease.

"Not as big a one as you gave me," she replied. "Goodness, Sophie, what are we do to?"

"To do?" Ian scratched his head. "Actually, you look all right to me now, love. It's probably nothing sinister, just a combination of hot weather and low blood sugar. I know what you girls can be like, skipping meals. Did you eat a decent breakfast before you came to work? I bet you haven't eaten anything all day."

I gave a hollow laugh. "A few minutes ago, I gave her a huge piece of millionaire's shortbread."

Ella was staring at him unseeingly. "Actually, Ian, it was the effect of shock. Shock at finding a dead body in the lost property cupboard."

Had Ella known about the dead body before I did? She must have done – that would explain why she had been so angry with me for looking in the lost property cupboard, and why she hadn't sounded particularly surprised when I told her what I'd found. Then there was her reaction to the shortbread – usually she'd have wolfed it down, but I wasn't sure she'd eaten any of it. Finding a dead body doesn't do a lot for the appetite.

Ian rolled his eyes. "Oh, that. Yes, Sophie told me. So, what was it in the end, Sophie? A big stray dog? A misplaced cow?"

I wasn't sure how to break it to him.

"Actually, Ian, maybe it's best if you go and see the dead body for yourself. I'm not sure I can bear to see it again. Then come back and tell us what you think we ought to do next."

As Ian trudged back into the building, leaving me and Ella sitting on the grass, I realised my hands were shaking.

"Whatever Ian thinks," I began slowly, "I guess the next thing is to call 999. Should we ask for police and ambulance, or just police?"

"I can't see what good an ambulance would do," said Ella. "He's definitely dead."

I was glad Ella at least had seen what I'd seen. Ian's flippant attitude wasn't helping.

"I suppose they'll need an ambulance to take him to the hospital morgue for a post-mortem." I shivered. "Considering we're sitting in the full sun on a hot July day, I don't feel very warm." I turned my face to the sunshine. "I don't suppose the school health and safety

19

policy includes an official protocol for dealing with dead bodies?"

"Nope, sorry." Ella plucked a daisy from the grass and began to pull off its petals one by one. "It's not a regular occurrence, you know."

"Maybe it would help if I ran up the road for Bob?" I suggested. "He could tell us what to do until the proper police get here."

To be fair, Bob is a proper policeman, too, but he works nights in the local constabulary headquarters in Bristol, so we never see him on duty. The only uniform I've seen him wear is a Keystone Kops fancy dress outfit in the carnival at the previous summer's Village Show.

Ella bit her lip. "Actually, I don't really want to see Bob just now. Nothing to do with the current circumstances, but, you know…"

She gazed at me like a naughty spaniel hoping to be forgiven for rolling in fox poo. Another reason I don't like dogs.

I clapped my hand over my mouth. "Oh, Ella! Surely you haven't been dating Bob? He must be twice your age."

She sighed. "I know, but he was so sweet when he came into school to talk to the kids about road safety, I didn't like to say no when he asked me out. Besides, it was only supper at The Bluebird, then a nightcap at his place. Hardly what I'd call a date."

She looked away.

"And was breakfast included?"

She put a forefinger to her lips. "Shh! Don't tell Ian! I don't want to lose his respect."

She pointed. Ian was strolling back towards us, frowning. When he reached us, he stopped and put his hands on his hips, towering over us.

"What are you two on about? There's no dead body in the lost property cupboard. There's nothing there but a pile of jumble. It's even more of a mess now that I've turned it upside down, hunting for a make-believe corpse. Honestly, I know the kids were getting silly towards the end of the summer term with their daft pranks, but I don't expect practical jokes from you two. Now, if you'll excuse me, I'll get back to my toilets, where I might find more sense."

As he marched off, swinging his arms, Ella and I stared at each other.

"Ella, I swear there was a dead body." I was beginning to doubt myself now. "You saw him too, didn't you, before I got here? I felt him and –" I shuddered. "He was as cold as a raw chicken from the village shop's chiller cabinet. There's no way he was alive. Unless some prankster had the foresight to stick his hands in the fridge before lying down to play dead?"

"Yes… yes, I did see him," Ella admitted slowly, "and it wasn't Tommy Crowe, if that's what you're thinking."

Tommy would be prime suspect for a stunt like that around the village. The previous autumn at the vicar's Guy Fawkes Night party, the mischievous teenager had played dead beneath an unlit bonfire, frightening the life out of us when he suddenly leapt to his feet.

Ella shrugged. "I suppose there's only one way to find out. Let's go and see for ourselves. Unlike Ian, we know what we're looking for."

"OK, Ella, let's do this."

I got to my feet and reached for her hands to haul her up. Ignoring the workmen's banter – or rather, heckles from Dai and hushes from his mates – we retraced our steps to the lost property cupboard. Ian had left the doors wide open and hauled its entire contents out onto the

21

floor of the entrance hall. There was no doubt about it. The dead body was no longer there.

4 Vanishing Act

"Let's be rational about this," said Ella, once we were back in her office. "It can't just have vanished."

She handed me a coffee from her machine before dropping in a fresh capsule to make a cup for herself. "Unless, of course, it wasn't really there in the first place."

I clasped my hands around the mug, glad of the warmth. My fingers were ridiculously cold with delayed shock, now that the adrenaline had stopped flowing.

"But you know it was there. You saw it before me, didn't you, which is why you were short with me when you realised I'd been in the cupboard." She looked away. "So we both saw it. You saw it first before I arrived, then I saw it. That's why you fainted, because you realised I'd seen it, too. Or was your faint a bluff? Were you playing for time while you tried to work out what to do about it?"

She remained silent, avoiding eye contact.

I wasn't giving up. "Am I right?"

She didn't speak until the coffee machine had stopped whirring.

"OK, you've rumbled me. But that doesn't mean I wasn't in a state of shock. All morning, I've been feeling as shaken as a butterfly in a thunderstorm."

"What? But when I arrived, you were cavorting to pop music in your office. That's tantamount to dancing on the poor guy's grave. Don't tell me... Don't tell me you killed him?"

She spluttered into her coffee.

"Sophie! I can't believe you just said that. Honestly, I know I get through a lot of men, but I always leave them with a pulse."

In spite of the severity of our dilemma, I laughed. I really needed to laugh.

Ella continued. "That's why I was playing my music so loud. When I discovered the body, I managed to keep my reaction bottled up until I got back to my office, but then I needed to mask my screams, and my sobs."

I reached across the desk to squeeze her trembling hands.

"Ella, I'm sorry."

"Then you barged in, banging on about library books, and I had to pretend everything was hunky dory and eat a big cake despite feeling sick as a child on a school coach trip."

I took a sip of coffee to moisten my parched mouth.

"Why didn't you tell me? I'm your friend. I'd have helped you."

She sighed. "In case you accused me of murder, like you just did."

I grimaced. "I'm sorry, Ella, I didn't mean it."

"Apology accepted. And I'm sorry I was so offhand with you this morning. I'd better explain why I was trying to get rid of you. The thing is, if word gets out that we have a dead body in school, all the parents will withdraw their kids immediately and enrol them at a different school for the new academic year. Believe me, all the other village schools around here would welcome our pupils with open arms. I don't know if you've noticed, but four years ago, there was a drop in the local birth rate, so there are very few four-year-olds about at the moment. That means a reduced reception class cohort for primary schools this autumn term. Now all the local village schools, whose rolls are small in any case, are trying to recruit new pupils from each other's catchment areas. It's a nightmare."

"But I thought Wendlebury was the best primary school around here?"

"Yes, and I'm the best at recruiting, so our reception class will be full, but only at the expense of the other schools. If they don't bump their numbers up over the next twelve months, the council is likely to close at least one of us and merge the two with the lowest numbers."

"But if Wendlebury School is best, surely they won't close it. You'll still have your job."

Ella slammed her mug down on her desk so hard that the pens in her pencil pot rattled.

"They might if it gets out that we're also a part-time morgue. It's just as well Ian didn't see the body. He's a terrible gossip. And as for those dreadful workmen –"

I stared into my coffee.

"I see what you mean. Once the police show up, word will be around the village like a flash flood. Whenever any emergency service vehicle is parked outside anyone's house, everyone starts speculating what's happened and won't rest until they find out. But perhaps it would be better to let people know the truth rather than allow Chinese whispers? Before the news reaches the end of the village, it'll be you that killed the workmen with the pneumatic drill."

Ella ran a hand over her eyes.

"Don't give me ideas."

She stood up to open the sash window, which I now realised had been closed to mask the sounds of her distress as well as her music. Then she sat down again, rubbed her hands together and turned to a fresh page in her notebook.

"Still, it's gone now. Problem solved. Maybe whoever it belonged to came back to claim it. That's how a lost property cupboard is meant to work, isn't it? Things get lost, and then they are found, and the rightful owner takes them away."

She picked up her pen and headed a clean sheet 'to do'. Aghast, I slapped my hand down on the page to prevent her writing.

"Ella, what are you thinking? Of course you have to call the police. Ignoring a dead body would be perverting the course of justice. We would be concealing evidence."

Calmly, she numbered the back of my hand 1, 2, 3.

"What evidence? There is no evidence."

I withdrew my hand.

"Of course there is. We both saw it. We have to report it. Then the police must search the cupboard for clues and swab it for fingerprints and DNA. But I'm sure if you ask them, they'll be discreet. It's not as if it's term-time. There won't be any parents or staff or kids to see them in action. If anyone asks why there was a police car at the school, you can say it was the road safety advisors following up Bob's visit. Anyway, I don't suppose they'll take very long. It's such a small space. Besides, we can speed things up by giving them a description." I tapped her pad. "Come on, write this down: about six feet tall, light brown curly hair."

She stopped writing.

"Dark brown. And straight. Gelled as straight as this." She held up her pen by way of illustration.

"Wavy."

"Straight."

"OK, but light brown, not dark."

"I'll just put brown."

"Clean shaven."

"Apart from the moustache." She added 'tache'.

"There was no moustache or beard."

She underlined 'tache'.

"Yes, there was, because that's what made me realise he was the image —"

She clamped her lips together.

"The image of what, Ella?"

She relented.

"The image of my ex-boyfriend, Lawrence Byrne."

I sat up so straight that my chair rebounded from the force of my back.

"Really? Do you think it was Lawrence Byrne?"

She gazed out of the window for a moment. A horse's head, followed by the upper half of a young woman, moved slowly by. To my fevered mind, the school's high front wall had rendered eerie a perfectly normal village sight of a lady riding a horse.

"I didn't take the time to check all his distinguishing features. I didn't want to get too close. Besides, we split up at least five years ago. A lot of things can happen in five years."

I smirked. "You mean a lot of men have passed under the bridge since then?"

She gave a wry grin.

"To be honest, in any identity parade, I'd probably spot someone who looked like one of my old flames. Lawrence was one of the better ones, and I suppose I was partly keeping my distance from the dead body because I didn't want to discover that it was him. I mean, who'd want to kill a nice guy like Lawrence Byrne?"

I drained the last of my coffee. "I think that's the least of our problems right now. We must phone the police before we do anything else. The longer we leave it, the worse it makes us look."

I glanced at the wall clock. I needed to get back to Hector's House, too.

"OK, I'll call," said Ella at last. "But please stay here to give me moral support."

"All right," I replied. "And let's tape the conversation, too, as witness to our best intentions."

"Good idea," said Ella, setting her phone to speaker mode.

I pulled my phone from my pocket, pressed "record" on the voice recorder app, and announced the time and date, like they do in police interview rooms on television shows.

5 Cupboard Love

Hector looked up from his keyboard and smiled as I strolled back into the shop.

"All done?"

Propping open the front door was our cast-iron door stop in the shape of a pile of vintage books, which always reminds me of the roomful of old books in Hector's flat above the shop. Lately I'd been trying to encourage him to open a second-hand department as an additional source of income.

"Not exactly," I replied.

I glanced around the shop. It was still relatively quiet. The only customers were an elderly couple in the tearoom drinking coffee and poring over the newspaper crossword together, and a mother and toddler sharing a board book in the children's section.

"Can you join me in the stockroom for a minute, please, Hector?"

As we're the shop's only staff, we never usually go in there at the same time while there are customers on the premises. He glanced around.

"What, now?"

I nodded, lowering my voice. "Yes, I really need to see you alone for a moment."

He gave me a quizzical look, then his face lit up.

"OK, then. After you."

As soon as he had closed the door behind us, he reached out to draw me to him, assuming I'd just been after a surreptitious romantic interlude. When I pushed him away and held him at arm's length, he looked puzzled.

"There's a crisis," I whispered. "A crisis at the school. Tell me if you think I've done the right thing."

Ignoring his hurt expression, I related the morning's events. He let me reach the point at which I'd discovered Ella had seen the body too before he interrupted me.

"Why didn't you call for me? I'd have come up to protect you while you waited for the police to arrive."

I waved away his concern.

"Don't be silly, I was perfectly safe with Ella. Ian and the builders were on site, too, don't forget."

Hector frowned. "Who's to say one of those people wasn't the murderer?"

"Innocent until proven guilty in this country, Hector." I confess my heart started to beat a little faster at the notion that the killer might have been lurking somewhere in the school the whole time. "Besides, you're always telling me how important it is that the bookshop adheres to its published opening hours. Unscheduled closures lose customers. Anyway, the point is, when Ella finally phoned the police, they wouldn't take her seriously. They assumed she was one of the kids playing a prank. She'd put the phone on loudspeaker so I heard the whole conversation. Honestly, Hector, it was unbelievable. They kept saying things like, 'I see, love, so you want to report a sighting of the Invisible Man'. Then they offered to send an invisible detective."

Hector laughed. "I can *see* their point, if you *see* what I mean."

I groaned. "Honestly, you'd think they were the pranksters, not Ella. But I reckon towards the end of the call, their senior officer must have walked in, as they suddenly turned all brusque and serious. They told her to get off the line, or they'd charge her with wasting police time."

I paused for breath while Hector took this all in.

"So it's just you and Ella who think you saw a body? Not Ian? Not the builders?"

I nodded wearily.

"The builders are working outside and have no cause to go to the lost property cupboard."

"Maybe your body was one of the builders playing a practical joke, trying to frighten you. If so, it worked."

I wrinkled my nose.

"Possibly. They seem jokey types, especially the loud Welsh one."

"Or one of them might have been taken ill and gone to lie down in the cupboard to recover."

I thought for a moment. "But they were all present and correct when Ian took Ella outside. And anyway, it's an odd place to choose – it wouldn't be very comfortable, and the air is less than fresh. But I suppose it would be private. And dark. If one of them developed a migraine, a darkened room would be perfect."

"Or concussion. From a head injury while dismantling the old play equipment."

That sounded more likely.

"I noticed their hard hats were lying on the grass. I suppose they'd be too hot to wear in this heatwave."

"Even so, they should still wear them for safety's sake."

"But that doesn't alter the fact that none of the workmen were missing when we went outside." I ignored the niggly reminder in my head, telling me that there had been no body, dead or otherwise, in the cupboard when Ian went to check, so a practical joker would have had plenty of time after my alarming discovery to rejoin his mates.

As if reading my mind, Hector asked, "What does Ian think? Have you asked him outright if he saw anyone lying down in the cupboard?"

"Not exactly, but if he did see a body, he made a good job of pretending he hadn't."

"Is this Ian, leading light of the Wendlebury Players? Are you sure it wasn't him playing dead? Did you ever see the supposed corpse and Ian at the same time? Or it could be that he's a secret murderer. He's burly enough to scoop up the evidence and carry it away to hide."

Hector's tone was teasing now, but a chill ran through my body as I realised that Ian would have had the perfect opportunity to hide the body when Ella and I were out on the field and we sent him inside to look in the cupboard.

"When Ella fainted, he lifted her up as easily as a bag of rubbish. What's more, those rubber gloves he was wearing, supposedly for cleaning the boys' toilets, will have stopped him leaving fingerprints."

6 Business Matters

I headed for the stockroom door.

"I think I'd better go back to the school and check on Ella."

Hector grabbed my hand to detain me.

"Not on your own, Sophie, please." I pulled my hand free, although gratified that he was starting to believe the body was real after all. "Not with the possibility of a killer on the loose. I mean, I'm sure there isn't, and there's most likely a rational explanation for what you think you saw. But let's establish that for certain before you take any risks."

I laid my hands on his shoulders and fixed him with what was meant to be a reassuring gaze.

"Which is exactly why I want to go and check on Ella now. Safety in numbers."

Hector bit his lip.

"Girl power," I added, trying to put from my mind the image of Ian smuggling a dead Ella out of the building in a rolled-up rug, like Cleopatra.

Hector took my hands in his and lifted them to his lips.

"I tell you what, let me go, just in case there really are any dangerous strangers lurking at the school. I know Ella's not expecting me, but I can easily rustle up some pretext for my visit." Glancing around the stockroom, he grabbed the first children's book he saw: Erich Kästner's *Emil and the Detectives*. "Here, I'll say I forgot to put this book in the order you delivered this morning."

Now I was picturing Ian lifting Hector off his feet and throwing him over his shoulder, before burying him in the mountain of grass cuttings at the bottom of the field. It would be a great place to hide a body, unlikely to be disturbed by anyone other than the person emptying the lawnmower.

Hector dropped my hands and consulted his wristwatch.

"Actually, it's nearly noon now, which means that shortly we'll both be able to leave the shop with a clear conscience."

"Why? What's happening at noon? Surely you're not introducing lunchtime closing? That's one of the most lucrative times for the tearoom."

"Ah, yes, well, there's something I've been meaning to tell you."

I said nothing, hoping to force him to fill the silence. My ploy worked.

"You see, after midday, we'll have an extra pair of hands. A new team member."

I sighed.

"Not Tommy, please. Don't tell me you've given in to his pleading for a holiday job. Tommy, who thinks all books look the same. Tommy, who can't tell Terry Pratchett from Charles Dickens. Besides, can you afford a third salary, even a teenager's minimum wage?"

"Good Lord, no. I've found someone far more suitable than Tommy; I've appointed a proper assistant."

I slumped down on the big chair by the desk I use to coach children with their reading skills after school in term-time. Hector has allowed me to turn a corner of the stockroom into a teaching area.

"A proper assistant?" I didn't mean to screech, but that's how it came out.

"Shhh! You'll frighten the customers."

He nodded towards the door, a finger to his lips. I tried again, this time my voice barely a squeak.

"What do you mean, a *proper* assistant? What's wrong with the one you've got? Me!"

He settled down into the chair beside mine, a smaller one for children, giving me the psychological advantage of looming over him.

"Nothing's wrong with you, sweetheart, but I was doing a lot of thinking while you were in Greece."

Surely he hadn't decided that I was dispensable? I was only gone for a week.

"While you were away, I realised you were right about my curiosities upstairs. I've decided to add a second-hand department to Hector's House – I'm going to call it Hector's Curiosities Shop. It'll be online at first, so we don't need an extra person to man it, but on the critical path is cataloguing the books and setting up sales pages for each one. Neither of us has time to do that, so I've organised an extra pair of hands."

"And whose hands are those?"

Hector's shoulders relaxed a little.

"Oh, you'll like her, she's a lovely girl."

Hating her already, I pasted a smile on my face.

"Is she local? I remember when you appointed me, you said how keen you were to employ a villager."

He wrinkled his nose. "Local-ish. She's from Hutmarton. She's just finished her A Levels at Slate Green Secondary School, and while you were away in Greece, she came in on spec, asking about a summer holiday job. She's been studying English literature, history of art and computing, which struck me as the perfect mix for appreciating old books while being technically savvy. The two months she has free before starting university should give her plenty of time to catalogue the books and populate the sales pages of our website. Even better, she's volunteered to work for free to gain experience and a reference."

"So she'll be an intern? I don't approve of asking anyone to work for free."

Hector's face fell.

"I thought you'd be pleased. Anyway, it's all agreed now. She starts today at noon. She's already till trained; she stayed for an hour when she visited so that I could show her the ropes."

"Why does she need to know how to use the till if she's only here to catalogue your old books?"

He shrugged. "She offered, and it seemed like a good idea. And she picked it up in no time. But don't look so glum, Sophie. It means if we ever want to leave the shop together, she can cover for us. Like today."

He paused, waiting for my reaction. I sensed that whatever I said would make no difference.

"So why didn't you tell me before?"

As I said it, I realised I would have been upset if it had been the first thing he had told me on my return from Greece, rather than how much he'd missed me. (He'd done a good job of that.) But he'd had two months since then to drop it into the conversation. There really was no excuse, but there was an explanation: he knew I'd be displeased.

He looked away, staring at the pile of empty cardboard boxes that were waiting for Tommy to come to flatten them for recycling, the only line of work Tommy can be trusted with at Hector's House. We pay him for it in milkshakes. I wondered what else had happened at the intern's interview. Had Hector got her tiddly on his hooch, same as he had me? Was she even old enough to drink alcohol?

Hector was still fumbling for an answer to my question.

"Well, time just flies, doesn't it? We're always so busy in the shop. It hasn't been front of mind until today." Perhaps sensing he was making a feeble case, he changed tack. "Besides, it's my decision to make. No disrespect, Sophie, but Hector's House is my business. We're not in partnership. You're my employee –"

As he faltered, I rose to my feet, glaring down on him in his little chair. He put his head in his hands, murmuring, "Hector, when you're in a hole, stop digging."

Before I could reply, there came a rap at the stockroom door.

"Hello?" The voice was female, young, girlish, but not a child's. "Hello, Mr Munro? Are you in there? It's me, Anastasia."

He hadn't even bothered to tell me her name. I decided to show him no mercy.

"Well, Mr Munro, while you attend to your new employee, I'm going to school to check on my friend."

Unwilling to reveal to the new girl how much her appointment had upset me, I fled via the back door of the stockroom and around the building towards the High

37

Street. If Anastasia was so multi-talented, she could manage the lunchtime rush in the tearoom, too.

7 About Turn

By the time I turned onto the High Street, I was regretting being so harsh on Hector, not to mention his new intern. Here she was in her first job, so lacking in self-esteem that she'd offered her services for free. She was probably a bag of nerves, and I was doing nothing to help.

Sisterhood, Sophie! I admonished myself. After all, it wasn't her fault that Hector was being a dolt. Instead of marching past the front door, I stepped inside it. Besides, I wanted to see whether this Anastasia looked as fancy as her name.

Hector, back at his usual post behind the trade counter, started as I came in, obviously not expecting me to appear at the front door.

"Sophie! What are you doing out in the street? Have you cloned yourself?" His jokey tone didn't fool me. My abrupt departure had unnerved him.

He glanced over to the tearoom where there stood a beautiful girl with big brown eyes and a thick, perfect fishtail plait nestling down her slender back like chocolate on an eclair.

"I don't know," he continued, "it strikes me that bookshop assistants are like buses. You wait for ages, then two come along at once. Ha-ha!"

Lumping me together with a teenage intern wasn't helping his cause.

"Anastasia's already pulling her weight by covering for you in the tearoom," he added.

But wasn't her job cataloguing the curiosities, not taking over my territory? Even so, I decided to be the grown-up here, and I gave her my friendliest smile.

"Anastasia, welcome to Hector's House. Hector's told me so much about you." As I spoke, I avoided looking in his direction, but I hoped he was cringing. "I hear you're hot stuff on the till, so I don't suppose you'll mind covering the trade counter while I borrow Hector for ten minutes?" He probably hadn't planned to give her quite so much responsibility on her first day, but he could hardly refuse my request.

Anastasia's heart-shaped face lit up, all dimples and cheekbones.

"No, of course not, Sophie. That would be fun, if Mr Munro thinks it's OK?"

"Oh, call him Hector, please!"

Hector spluttered. "Yes, do call me Hector. You're not at school now."

"Righto, Hector," Anastasia said sweetly. "See you later then, Sophie."

So she was nice too. How very annoying.

In silence, Hector followed me into the street.

"OK, OK, I'm sorry, Sophie. I should have told you sooner about Anastasia. If I'd known you were going to have such a traumatic morning, I certainly would have done things differently."

We fell into step as we approached the school entrance. When Hector took my hand and I didn't pull it away, he became more courageous. He gave an uncertain smile.

"You're not jealous, are you? After all, she's not much older than Tommy."

"About four years older than Tommy," I pointed out. "And in terms of maturity, about ten years his senior. For heaven's sake, Hector, she's a young woman. Anyway, enough about Anastasia. Don't let her distract us from Ella and her dead body."

I punched the entry code into the school's front door and opened it to find Ian bagging up the contents of the lost property cupboard. He looked up as we arrived and gave a sheepish grin.

"I've told Ella that next time she wants me to empty the lost property cupboard, she should just ask me nicely, instead of inventing nonsense about dead bodies. It is not as if I ever refuse her anything." He pointed to a dozen library books stacked neatly on the trophy cupboard. "Sophie, these are for you. I've wiped them all down with an antibacterial cloth, so you don't have to worry about catching anything when you put them back in the library. I'm guessing that's what you've come to do now?" He turned to Hector. "Is tidying the school library a two-man job or is this a staff outing?"

Hector cleared his throat. "No, I just wanted a bit of fresh air. It's so stuffy in my shop and much cooler in here. I don't have the advantage of a through draught like you do." He nodded towards the French doors leading onto the playground. They were now propped open with fire extinguishers. "So I thought I'd come and inspect the work on the new playground. My shop sponsored one of the benches, you know."

I'd already knocked on Ella's office door.

"I'll tell Ella we're here, Hector, while you take a look outside. Come and find me when you're done."

This time, Ella's office was silent, but for the tapping of a computer keyboard. When she called, "Come in", I detected a tremor in her voice. As I entered, she pushed her keyboard away and sat back in her chair. I doubted her mind was on her work.

"Can't keep away, can you?" she joked, but her expression was sombre.

I closed the door behind me so we could talk without being overheard, but as she still had her window open, I kept my voice low.

"Ian thinks I've come to tidy the library and that Hector's come to see where his sponsored bench is going, but we've really come about you-know-what."

"So who's minding the shop?"

I grimaced. "Anastasia, our new intern."

She welcomed the diversion.

"An intern? I've never known Hector get an intern before. Until you arrived last summer, it's always just been Hector at the bookshop, with Kate bailing him out now and again for the odd dental appointment or book fair. Isn't having an intern a bit grand for his little shop?"

I sat down on her visitor's chair, which she took as a cue to make us coffee.

"To be honest, her appointment was a surprise to me too, but apparently she came into the shop while I was away in Greece, offering her services for free between A Levels and university."

Ella dropped a capsule into the machine.

"An eighteen-year-old, eh? Is she pretty? Have you got competition?"

42

There was no point pretending. She'd find out soon enough.

"She looks like a young Greek goddess. She seems very sweet, too, damn her."

Ella wrinkled her nose. "You'd better watch your step."

Irritating though her comment was, at least it assured me that Ella had regained her equilibrium. However, I hadn't come here to discuss Anastasia. Gently, I steered Ella back to the mysterious dead body. I nodded towards the entrance hall.

"Ian thinks the dead body was a ruse of yours to get him to empty the lost property cupboard. Do you think we should disabuse him of that belief?"

She slumped forward in her chair, put her elbows on her desk and let her head fall into her hands.

"What can we do in the absence of any evidence? You heard what the policeman said to me. He wasn't just dismissive, he was threatening."

I leaned across her desk and lowered my voice still further, mindful of the open window.

"We could go looking for the dead body, on the assumption that it might still be somewhere on the premises."

Ella shrank back in her seat.

"No, Sophie. I don't want to find it, and you can't make me look for it. Good riddance, if you ask me." She got to her feet. "I'll just go and butter up Hector about his bench – I need to keep in with the school's donors – and then we can get on with what we are meant to be doing this afternoon: you tidying up the library and me doing my end of term accounts."

She was right. The school was her domain, and I couldn't force her to do anything here. But her fear for

43

the school's reputation was not going to prevent me from making discreet investigations on my own.

I followed her out into the entrance hall where she detached Hector from his conversation with Ian and escorted him outside, while I took the stack of rescued books to the glorified cupboard that serves as the school library.

The Victorian building is full of nooks and crannies and closets, and the school has to be creative to make the antiquated design serve twenty-first century educational needs. There were plenty of places where a body might be hidden by someone who knew their way around the place. I caught my breath as I opened the library door, half expecting to find the dead body among the bookshelves, or perhaps beneath them, its huge trainers sticking out like the witch's red shoes in *The Wizard of Oz*.

But all was well. The tiny room was just a little musty in the absence of any source of fresh air, apart from a couple of small skylights at the top of the wall. From the corner, I seized the long wooden pole with the hook on it, the only means to open those high windows.

Even the small amount of fresh air they admitted came as a relief, and I set about tidying the shelves. While I considered Ella's dilemma, I started placing all the books the right way up, spines outwards, before checking they were in Dewey Decimal System order. Which, of course, they weren't, thanks to slapdash library monitors, demob-happy in their final term.

I'd reached 520 (Astronomy) when a tap at the door startled me.

"Everything OK, sweetheart?"

Hector came in and closed the door behind him. Having spent the past five minutes crouched by the lowest shelf, I was glad of the excuse to straighten up. As

I stretched my arms above my head, arching my back, Hector ran a hot fingertip down my spine.

"All good here. How about you? Did you notice anything suspicious outside? Did Ella say anything about the body? How do you think she seemed in herself?"

"Nothing to report, and Ella seemed OK, just a bit tense, as if she was on her best behaviour. But my chat with Ian was interesting."

He lowered his voice.

"He reckons that the pressure to fill the reception class for the autumn, on top of the stress of managing everything in Mrs Broom's absence, has got a bit too much for Ella. He also told me that he thinks she's unlucky in love and – I'm using his words – that 'another wretch has broken her heart'. Bob, apparently."

He paused to gauge my reaction.

"Policeman Bob?" I squealed. He hushed me and said yes.

"Sorry," I whispered. "But she told me she'd dumped Bob unceremoniously after a one-night stand. Her heart was not involved in the equation."

Hector frowned. I suspected his sympathies lay with Bob. "I'm glad I've always steered clear of a date with her."

It wasn't the first time I had been relieved Hector had had a long dry spell after his last serious girlfriend left him before he took up with me. How awkward if he were one of Ella's cast-offs.

"You know, Sophie, Ian thinks Ella is without fault. But I bet if he thought she had done something wrong, he'd cover for her."

I reached out to straighten a disorderly row of junior dictionaries on the top shelf.

"You mean you think she's the murderer and Ian's in on it with her? Of course not! She's one of my best friends!"

Hector shrugged.

"How convincing was her funny turn? Might it have been staged to distract you? Perhaps she didn't really faint, and when Ian was carrying her outside, she whispered to him to hide the body while she detained you in the playground. Or she could have said something to him while you were talking to the workmen."

I considered for a moment, remembering that I too suspected Ella's faint had been less than genuine.

"I don't know. It goes against all my instincts to mistrust her. But you're right, we must keep our minds open to all possibilities. Here's another idea: maybe Ian's really in love with her and murdered one of her boyfriends in a fit of jealousy, or even at her command, and now they're collaborating to cover it up. Ella knew there was a corpse in the cupboard before I arrived this morning and she didn't want me to see it."

I shuddered as I used the word corpse. It made it seem more real and more criminal.

Hector's eyes widened.

"You don't think the corpse could have been Bob, do you? When he's on permanent night shift, he could be missing for days before anyone noticed."

My heart missed a beat at the suggestion. I liked Bob. But then my common sense recalibrated it.

"You're forgetting I saw the body's face. It definitely wasn't Bob. It was no one I had ever seen before in my life. Whether the same is true for Ella, I really don't know. She admitted he looked like an old flame, but she didn't absolutely say if he was or wasn't."

Suddenly, Hector grinned. "Oh, Sophie, listen to us! A pair of writers with overactive imaginations! I'm sorry, sweetheart, but I think Ian's right. Call it a mirage, if you like. Goodness knows, it's hot enough for a mirage."

I didn't really know what to believe now, but how could I disbelieve what I'd seen with my own eyes?

A distant crash and a scream made us both gasp.

Hector flung open the library door, and I raced after him in the direction of the disturbance: Ella's office. Ian stood framed in the open doorway with his back to us, a weapon in his hand.

"Don't worry, love, I'll clear that up for you," he was saying.

When he turned around at the sound of our approach, I realised the 'weapon' was only a dustpan and brush. Ella, kneeling on the floor beside her desk, looked up at us in surprise.

"What are you two gawping at? It's only a cup of coffee."

And with that, she burst into noisy tears.

8 Ella's Escort

"I think I'd better take you home, love," said Ian, sweeping the fragments of broken china into the dustpan on the floor beside Ella's desk. "You're exhausted. You need a rest. Just let me empty my dustpan into the bin, then I'll fetch my car. You're in no fit state to drive."

Still kneeling on the floor, Ella curled up into a ball, as if trying to make herself as small as possible. As she began to sob into her lap, I crouched down to slip my arms around her.

"Don't worry, Ella, you'll feel better after a rest. There's nothing here that can't wait until tomorrow. Let Ian take you home, have a quiet evening in, and start afresh in the morning."

"I could run her home if you like, Ian," said Hector. "I suppose you should stay on site as you're the only other member of school staff here."

Ian rolled his eyes. "Don't you start. You sound like Mrs Broom." He raised his voice an octave in a skilful imitation of the headteacher. "'A caretaker should take more care.' I'd like to see her manage all the tasks I get through in a day, while she's holed up in her fancy office drinking posh coffee."

48

'Fancy' was putting it strongly, but it was a pretty room in a cottagey way, twice the size of Ella's office.

"Same goes for Ella," Ian went on. "Mrs Broom's making her work so hard that she's starting to hallucinate."

I glanced down at Ella, trying to assess her take on his statement, but she kept her face hidden from view.

"I saw it too, Ian," I began, but Ian just tutted.

"Mass hysteria," he said in a low voice to Hector. "Heightened suggestibility of a writer's imagination."

Hector gave a nervous laugh. Ian had no idea of Hector's secret identity as a successful romantic novelist, and Hector wanted to keep it that way.

Ella's sobbing subsided.

"Sophie, could you drive me home?"

I shook my head. "Sorry, Ella, you're forgetting I can't drive."

At last she uncurled herself and sat back on her heels.

"But you need to get back to your shop, Hector," she told him. "We've taken up too much of your time. Sophie told me about your new intern. You can't leave her at the helm on her first day. Talk about throwing her in at the deep end."

Now I thought of it, where had Anastasia been all morning? If she was meant to be working full-time, why had she not come to the shop until noon? Might she have had anything to do with our vanishing body?

While Ian emptied his dustpan into Ella's bin, I helped my friend to her feet. Once she'd powered down her computer, closed the window and picked up her bag, she allowed Ian to lead her out of her office, his arm around her shoulders. On the threshold, Ian turned to me.

"Sophie, could you please stay here till I get back? That way I won't have to bother setting the alarms or locking

49

everything up. And you never know, the builders might need to come in to use the loo."

Caretaker, take more care, I thought, as he left without waiting for an answer.

***

Once Hector had left for the shop, and I was the only one in the school building, I was too nervous to return to the glorified cupboard that was the school library. So I closed the front door behind Hector and wandered out onto the playing field for some fresh air. Even the company of those cheeky workmen was preferable to being indoors alone. Besides, I might check them out now for any signs of suspicious behaviour in relation to the disappearing dead body.

If Hector's theory was correct, and the body had merely been one of the workmen, now that I'd calmed down, I should be able to recognise which one. And if I did, I could ask them what they were playing at: a practical joke, a quiet snooze, or recovering from a blow to the head? If it had been the last option, it was in their best interests to log it in the school accident book. If they incurred lasting harm, they would most likely be eligible to claim for damages from the school's insurance policy. Why would they not report an accident?

I noticed their white van was unmarked. Maybe they were an unofficial business operating without insurance against industrial accidents? That would reduce their overheads so that they could offer more competitive prices, but only at great risk to themselves. It was probably also illegal.

As I crossed the tarmacked playground, for once not tempted to hopscotch on the painted grid, Dai put down his spade and grinned at me.

"Aye aye, come back for the real men now you've shaken off Hercule Poirot? Meet my mates Robbie and Matt."

"Hercule Poirot?"

Dai's mates lowered their spades too, no doubt glad of an excuse to take a break beneath the scorching midday sun.

"You know, Hercule, that curly-headed laddie who was prowling about earlier."

"Head like a stick of candyfloss," added Robbie helpfully.

I bit my lip to hide my amusement at this unflattering description of my boyfriend's dark curls.

"His name's Hector, and he wasn't prowling. His business made a donation to the playground, so he just came to see how things are progressing." I nodded at their idle spades. "Not much, by the look of it."

Their comments reminded me to compare their hair with the corpse's. Dai's was shaven, Robbie's was a shaggy dark blond and Matt's a receding grey stubble. I hoped Dai and Matt had applied suncream, or else they'd end up redheads, literally. Robbie was thus the only candidate. Although Ella and I had disagreed on the exact nature of the body's hair, he'd definitely had some. What looked light blond in bright sunshine might easily pass for mid or dark brown in the gloom of the lost property cupboard. Robbie's unkempt locks might be described as wavy or curly.

If they'd been wearing their hard hats, I wouldn't have been able to see any of the workmen's hair at all, so it worked in my favour that they had taken them off and flung them on the grass. There were no bumps to suggest recent concussion on either Dai or Matt's heads, but Robbie could easily have concealed an injury beneath his dense thatch.

I tried to picture him lying down in the shade with his eyes and mouth closed. I wanted to believe it had been him in the cupboard, as that would be the happiest outcome I could imagine from the morning's events.

"You'll recognise me again, love," Robbie was saying, and I realised I'd been staring at him.

"Sorry, I just had a feeling you might be someone I know."

He grinned. "We can soon make that happen, love. I'm footloose and fancy free just now. How about you?"

"Actually, Hector is my partner. My boyfriend, I mean. We also work together in our bookshop on the High Street."

I wasn't going to tell them it was his bookshop and he was my boss. I wanted to project an air of authority.

Dai laughed. "Then I guess we'll have to call you Miss Marple, my lovely. You got the frock for it. You borrowed it off your granny?"

It was just as well Matt interrupted before I could reply. "They're not an item, Poirot and Marple."

"You're thinking of Mulder and Scully in *The X Files*," put in Robbie. "Cor, that Agent Scully's a looker – or is it Agent Mulder? I can never remember which is which."

Before the conversation could descend any further, I decided to press on with my investigation.

"By the way, while I'm here, I don't suppose you've seen anyone else on the premises this morning, apart from Ella, Ian, Hector and me? You see, we've lost someone who might have been a little disoriented, possibly suffering from concussion."

That none of them flinched rather spiked Hector's theory that the body had been one of them.

"What sort of person, love?" asked Dai. "One of the kids?"

"Not unless it was a child with a five o'clock shadow," I replied, only realising now that the body I'd seen wasn't clean shaven, despite what I'd said to Ella.

"My word, kids grow up fast round here, don't they?" replied Dai.

"Must be all that fertiliser on the fields," added Robbie, "getting into your water."

Realising I wasn't going to get any more sense out of them, I consulted my watch and remarked upon the time.

Matt picked up his shovel. "Come on, lads, look lively. Here comes the Jolly Green Giant to check up on us."

I turned to see Ian's car pulling into the car park. I gave the workmen one last shot.

"Well, if you do remember anything you think might be relevant to our missing friend – a grown man, by the way – do come and let me know. You know where to find me: Hector's House, the bookshop on the High Street. I run the tearoom, and if you can find our missing man, there'll be free tea and a cake in it for you."

That perked them up.

"Tearoom? Why didn't your curly friend tell us about your tearoom?" asked Robbie.

Dai wafted his fingers over his forehead like Madame Arcati. "Ah, I think I feel a recollection coming on! Save us a chocolate brownie, please, love, just in case."

9 Taking Care of Business

Ian was just coming in through the front door as I reached the entrance hall.

"Thanks for holding the fort, Sophie. Ella seemed calmer once she was in her flat. It's a nice place she's got there."

I nodded. "I just hope she'll be OK on her own. I'll give her a call later, and if she wants company, I'll get Hector to drop me over there after work."

Ian grabbed his brown duster coat from where he'd left it on top of the trophy cabinet and slipped it on. I was glad I didn't have to wear an extra layer in this heat; I didn't blame him for taking it off at every opportunity.

"Don't worry, Sophie. Ella will be all right for company. She said she was going to call her mum after I had gone. I expect her mum will come over if she needs her and might even stay the night."

"OK, well, I'll call her later anyway. Now I'd better get back to the shop. I'll finish sorting out the library another day, once Ella's back in."

***

As I entered Hector's House, Anastasia was serving an afternoon tea to Billy. She smiled as she saw me.

"I hope I've done it right?" She pointed at Billy's scones.

"No, girlie, you've forgotten my special cream," Billy protested.

I doubted Hector had let her into the secret of his special cream: a pale liqueur he distils in the stockroom to earn a little extra revenue.

"Don't worry, Anastasia, I'll take it from here," I said quickly. "Now Hector can get you set up with your proper job." Hearing his name, Hector, typing at the trade counter, looked up. "She's all yours, Hector. I'll cover the trade counter while you're gone."

Watching Hector lead Anastasia out the front door and around the corner, Billy forgot his complaint.

"'Ere, where's Hector taking that kiddie?"

If I didn't explain, the local rumour mill would invent a less accurate alternative in no time.

"Up to his flat. He's got a project up there he wants her to work on."

Billy chortled. "That's his story. You want to keep an eye on your fella, girlie. Not that she's much more than a schoolgirl, for all her cleavage and make-up."

I marched over to the fridge to fill a small jug with Hector's hooch and set it down beside Billy's teapot with more force than I intended.

"You don't seem very happy." Billy picked up his butter knife. "Should we be hiding sharp instruments in case you decide to get your revenge?"

"To be honest, Billy, I'm that cross I could do him significant damage with a teaspoon."

Billy's mischievous grin softened.

"Grab yourself a cup and saucer, then sit down and tell me all about it," he said gently. "I can't enjoy my tea if I thinks love's young dream's up the spout."

Despite his gruffness, Billy's heart is in the right place. As I fetched another cup, the only other customer left the shop without buying anything, and before I knew what I was doing, I was pouring my heart out to Billy. Goodness knows why. As a confirmed bachelor, he is hardly in the best position to offer romantic counselling.

He listened in silence, apart from his usual repertoire of noises that accompany the ingestion of his afternoon tea, as I explained about Anastasia's appointment.

"It sounds to me like Hector thought you'd be pleased," he said when I'd finished. "You've been on at him for ages to get his finger out about selling his old books, and now he's taking steps to do it, you're not happy. Shouldn't you be glad that you've got him under your thumb and he's doing what he's told?"

I sighed.

"I suppose so. But it would have bothered me less if he'd appointed a boy or a middle-aged person, rather than a beautiful young girl."

Billy licked his forefinger and ran it around his plate to capture the last crumbs.

"I daresay Hector never even noticed what she looks like. He most likely just sees a useful pair of hands and a young brain that's been operating computers since she was a babby – and a means of making you happy."

Billy's take on events made me start to feel better. At least, it did until Hector told me his side of the story after work.

10 Deceptive Appearances

"The thing is, I just liked the look of her."

As Hector flipped the door sign to closed, I pulled a hideous face to his back to get some of the anger out of my system.

"You're not helping your case, Hector."

He returned to the trade counter to start cashing up.

"What I mean is, I thought her face would fit in the shop. In our team line-up, I mean."

Releasing the catch to lift out the cash drawer and set it on the counter in front of him, he began to count the notes, not looking at me.

"So, we're a team now, are we? I thought you said I was just staff earlier?"

I stacked the cups up in the dishwasher.

"Of course we're a team, sweetheart, so don't you think it's important for any new person to fit into our dynamic?"

After wrapping an elastic band around the roll of notes, he started on the coins.

"Yes, but can't you see how it makes me feel to have Anastasia sprung on me? It would have been nice to meet her beforehand, or even to have been involved in her interview."

Having lost count of the pound coins in his hand, he slid them back onto the counter and started again.

"I just thought you'd like her. Besides, you weren't here when she came into the shop, you were off enjoying yourself in Greece."

"Yes, but I've been back two months. You could have told me any time since, and maybe invited her in to meet me in advance, rather than letting her turn up as a fait accompli."

"I didn't like to distract her during her A Levels."

I threw a dishwasher tablet into the machine and slammed the door shut.

"Cast your mind back, Hector. A Levels finish in June. Surely you can remember that long summer holiday when you finished school a month before all the younger classes? You're only a few years older than me. It's not that long ago even for you."

He slipped the pound coins into a bank bag and folded over the top.

"Oh yes, now you mention it. Still, she suggested starting at the beginning of the school holidays, and it made sense to me at the time. Plus it gave me the opportunity to get references from her teachers."

I hadn't thought about references. I didn't remember him asking for any at my job interview.

As I cleaned the sink, I thought back to the fateful day of my interview the previous summer. Hector had told me I was the only local applicant, but later I'd found a pile of discarded applications from other villagers in the paper recycling box. In the end, I'd worked out that it was my connection with May Sayers that had swung him. She had underwritten the costs of setting up his bookshop and, in addition to stocking her books (she was a travel writer), he felt employing me was an appropriate way to thank her posthumously for her kindness. His recruitment method was certainly unconventional.

So what was the deal with Anastasia? Stuffing the day's tea towels into my basket to take home to wash, I decided to let matters lie for a bit. After the events at the school, I probably wasn't at my most rational.

"So what hours is she going to do?"

At my conciliatory tone, Hector brightened.

"Ten till four with an hour for lunch, to tie in with the timetable for the Hutmarton bus."

He lifted the framed map of the parish down from the wall behind him and unlocked the safe it concealed.

"So why wasn't she here till noon today?"

"She said she had something she needed to do first."

He slid the till drawer into the safe.

"In Wendlebury?"

He shrugged.

"I don't know, I didn't think to ask. None of my business really. I assumed it was a doctor's appointment, or a home delivery she needed to wait in for."

He secured the safe and returned the picture to its hook.

"But the only morning bus that comes up from Hutmarton gets here at ten to ten. There isn't one at noon."

Hector came over to wash his hands at the basin behind the tearoom counter and gave them a cursory dry on his jeans. It was still warm enough for any remaining moisture to evaporate within seconds, but he finished drying them on my back, wrapping his arms round me for an after-hours hug.

"Anyway, enough about Anastasia. My chief concern is you. You've had a stressful day, thanks to Ella and her wild imaginings. How about you stay at mine tonight in case you have nightmares? I know how suggestible you are."

I leaned back just enough to look into his eyes.

"But it was there, Hector, the dead body really was there."

"Really? You mean you weren't just humouring Ella? Ian kept telling me how overworked she is and how much she carries her boss."

"So a bit like me, then." I rested back into his embrace. The physical comfort of a hug was very welcome after the strains of the day. "But yes please, an evening at yours would be lovely."

I wriggled free to pick up my basket, then I followed him to the front door. While he set the alarm and locked up, I waited outside.

"I don't think Ella should be alone, either. Ian said she was going to call her mum, but she might just have been saying that to get rid of him. Let's ring her this evening to check up on her. But first, I'll pop home to feed Blossom and put these tea towels in the washing machine. Want anything from the village shop?"

"Only you," he said with a smile. "Hurry back, sweetheart."

11 The Mysterious Letter

I was glad to get out of the heat of Hector's House and into the light, warm breeze wafting down the High Street.

When I stopped at the village shop, even with my sunglasses on, I could see that Carol Barker, serving behind the counter, was more than a little flushed. Although standing right by the open door, she had middle-age and bulk working against her, and a natural modesty that daunted her from dressing down for the weather.

"Aren't you a bit warm in that cardigan, Carol?" I asked, fetching a bottle of Vinho Verde from the far end of the shop where it was shelved between the Vimto soft drink and the Vosene shampoo. Carol is a stickler for alphabetical order.

She pulled an old-fashioned handkerchief from her cardigan pocket to wipe her brow.

"But it's pure cotton, Sophie. It's a summer cardigan."

I searched in my handbag for my purse.

"Yes, but it must be over 30 degrees even now. Surely you haven't been wearing it all day?"

She looked away.

"I don't want to put my customers off with my bare arms. Not at my age."

Without meaning to, I glanced at her arms, trying to assess what they'd look like without the cardigan.

"There's nothing wrong with your arms." Privately, I thought her customers – not to mention Ted, who'd been her boyfriend since the Valentine's event Ella and I had organised in The Bluebird – might be more put off by her damp scarlet face. "It's arduous enough being on your feet all day in this heat without being inappropriately dressed. That's why I've been absolutely living in Auntie May's old Indian dresses lately. They keep me so cool."

Carol ran a finger around the inside of the high neckline of her dress, which was sticking to her damp chest.

"They look lovely and airy on you, Sophie."

"Your dress isn't cotton, is it?" I asked.

She looked down at the floral print.

"No, it's polyester. But it's ever so easy to care for. You just wash it, hang it on the line, and you can put it on as soon as it's dry. No need for even the touch of an iron."

"I hope you're not ironing anything at the moment. In humid weather like this, any wrinkles will just fall out. Auntie May taught me that. She never took an iron on her travels."

"I wish the wrinkles would fall out of me," Carol said quietly, as she rang up my purchase on the till.

***

As I continued down the High Street, the scents of cottage garden flowers hung in the air. Roses and lavender, stocks and wallflowers: the perfect antidote to the cloying, sickly smell of the lost property cupboard, which hadn't quite left my nostrils yet.

Beside my front door, Auntie May's peonies were in full bloom. Since I'd left for work that morning, a few more of their tight green buds had unfurled into showy magenta clusters. I slid the key into the lock, and as I opened the door, the cool indoor air washed over me. Thick stone walls make these old Cotswold cottages cool in summer and warm in winter.

"Blossom!" I pushed my sunglasses onto the top of my head. "Blossom, Mummy's home!"

I never call myself Mummy when Hector's around, and not only because he's disdainful of cats. I don't want him to think I'm hinting about our future together.

When Blossom didn't appear, I scooped up the post from the doormat and took it through to my little kitchen. First things first: I popped the wine in the freezer to chill it down quickly, stuffed the tea towels in the washing machine, filled the detergent drawer and switched it on. Then I opened the back door and called again to my kitten.

When no response came, I braced myself to go back out into the heat, pulling my sunglasses down from the top of my head against the glare.

A distinctive chirrup came from halfway down the garden, where Blossom was basking in the sunshine. Her tummy was on the cool grass of the lawn, and her back pressed against the scorching drystone wall, retaining the warmth of the day like a storage heater. My late grandfather, an accountant, would have said that with her hot back and cool belly, on average, she was perfectly comfortable, and I think Blossom would have agreed.

Blossom's sole concession to my arrival was to narrow her eyes, the cat equivalent of a smile, and roll over onto her back.

"Hello, little one." As I stroked her sun-kissed tummy, she began a languorous purr.

"Hello to you, too." A deep wavery voice, enriched with a smile, came from behind me. I straightened up to see my elderly neighbour leaning on the gate in the wall that separates his garden from mine.

"Hello, Joshua."

He raised his battered Panama hat in greeting. I wondered whether Auntie May had brought it back from one of her trips to Central America. They'd been childhood sweethearts, separated for their adult lives until reuniting late in their old age.

"Hot enough for you, my dear?"

"More than hot enough, thanks. How are you coping with the heatwave?"

By rights, he should have been even hotter than Carol, in his customary long-sleeved shirt, dark tie, flannel trousers, knitted pullover and tweed jacket. Swapping his usual tweed cap for the Panama hat was his sole concession to the season.

"Hot weather never bothers me, my dear, I am just happy to be warm for a change. My circulation is not what it used to be. And you?"

I'd noticed he kept his wood burner blazing hotter and for longer than mine in the winter. At least there was no smoke rising from his chimney just now.

"It's been boiling in the bookshop, and Hector's flat won't be much better." I bit my lip; I never liked to admit to Joshua that I spent whole nights at Hector's flat for fear of shocking him. "I'm going back up for supper in a little while."

His eyes twinkled.

"Please give Hector my very best regards. Oh, and would you mind asking him whether he has any Longfellow in his private collection? I fancy spending some time in the company of Hiawatha. In my youth, I could recite the whole poem by heart. I noticed when I was last in the shop, Longfellow was absent from the poetry section. Perhaps he has fallen out of fashion. Only afterwards did it occur to me Hector might own a copy that I might borrow. Tomorrow will do, no rush for tonight."

I was glad about that.

After raising his hat once more, he pottered over to tend to the sweet peas rambling up a teepee of bamboo canes beyond his vegetable patch. Perhaps it was the teepee that had put him in mind of Hiawatha.

Blossom rolled over and got slowly to her feet. She stretched her front paws then her back, until she looked twice her usual length, before trotting to the kitchen door, where she stopped to look at me over her shoulder. I took the hint and went inside to decant some fresh wet food onto a saucer, before topping up her dishes of biscuits and water.

Filling a tumbler with iced water for myself, I sat down at the kitchen table to flick through my post – all fliers and circulars, apart from one small white envelope bearing my name in shaky capitals. I didn't recognise the handwriting.

A tap at the back door made me jump, and I looked up to find Joshua peering in, leaning on his stick with one hand and holding a bunch of pink and mauve sweet pea flowers in the other. Their heady fragrance entered the room before he did. Beckoning him inside, I held up the envelope to show him.

"This isn't from you, is it?"

He peered at it through the lower part of his bifocals.

"No, my dear. But these are, with my compliments."

He held out the sweet peas, and as I took them from him, my fingers brushed his papery skin, as cold as the ice in my drink. I filled one of May's old pressed-glass vases from the tap and held the blooms up to my nose before plunging the stems into the water.

"The scent will fill your cottage by bedtime," he said. "Enjoy it."

"Thank you, I will."

I smiled. Raising his hat as a parting gesture, he turned to go, before making his way slowly up the path to the gate between our gardens.

As soon as he was out of sight, I ran upstairs to freshen up in the shower, before slipping into a clean one of May's Indian frocks and the same strappy leather sandals I'd been wearing earlier. Ten minutes later, I was on my way to Hector's, swinging my French straw shopping basket, the chilled bottle of Vinho Verde providing a pleasing weight in the bottom. I'd slung in the mysterious letter to read later, not wanting to delay my return to Hector.

***

"I thought we might take a picnic up to the Cotswold Way," he said, as I appeared at the top of his stairs. He'd left the street door open for me. He had also changed his clothes, and his dark curls, now gleaming coils, bore witness to a recent shower. "That is, until I saw your fancy dress."

Playfully I slapped the seat of his khaki shorts, before giving a twirl, the full skirt of the dress creating a pleasing breeze about my legs.

"Yes, I've come as a woman of the world. Indian dress, Greek shoes, French shopping basket." With a flourish, I produced the cold bottle, now beaded with condensation. "And Portuguese wine." As I did so, a flash of white fluttered to the floor. Hector bent to pick the envelope up, glancing at the writing as he handed it to me.

"And Dutch spelling, at a guess?"

The correspondent had spelled my name with an f instead of ph. I realised now that I'd been wrong to assume it was an old person's handwriting, like Joshua's. Now that I looked at it properly, I could see no signs of a tremor; it was just untidy and awkward. Perhaps the sender was a person not used to writing in English, or maybe they wrote it while drunk. Having taught in a few international schools on mainland Europe before I moved to Wendlebury, I knew a lot of foreigners, but I didn't know any drunks.

"Do we have any Dutch people in Wendlebury?" I wondered, settling down on one of the high stools at the breakfast bar.

Hector scratched his head, making his damp curls bounce.

"Not that I know of, sweetheart. I think your name might be spelled that way in other languages, too. Could it be Russian?"

"No, silly, if it was in Russian, it would be in the Cyrillic alphabet."

I was hoping it wasn't German. My ex, Damian, had been living in Germany when I left him, and he'd never been great at spelling. Might this herald his return? After all, he had turned up in the village unannounced just before Christmas.

"Shall I open the wine while you read your letter?" Hector was saying. "I've put a bottle of sparkling red apple juice in with our picnic, but we could have a glass of wine now and finish the bottle on our return."

"On a school night?"

"Vinho Verde is quite low in alcohol. Besides, you're forgetting school's out for summer."

Another reminder I didn't need. In hope of distracting myself from my mental image of the dead body, I tore open the envelope. Inside was a sheet of old-fashioned notepaper, the sort Auntie May used when she wrote to me at university. Unlike her packed pages, this sheet had only a few words scrawled across it. As I read the message aloud, my heart began to pound.

"I know what happened to your aunt and you're next. From A Nun."

Wide eyed, I stared at Hector, who passed me the wine glass he had just filled. Auntie May had died the previous year.

"I didn't know there were any nuns in the village," I said. Taking a big swig, I pressed the glass against my burning cheeks.

After pouring a glass for himself, Hector put the bottle in the fridge and came round to sit on the stool beside mine. He took the letter when I held it out to him.

"No, there aren't. How very peculiar. She must have just been passing through. So we're looking for a possibly Dutch nun who knew May Sayers. On holiday, perhaps, if nuns have holidays. I suppose May met nuns on her travels."

I took a smaller sip of my wine.

"She certainly did. She occasionally stayed in convents when she wanted peace and quiet to finish a book. Some take paying guests, you know. She even wrote a book about convents. Maybe her book upset one of the nuns, and she's come to take it out on me."

Hector turned the sheet over, but there was nothing on the reverse.

"Yes, I remember it now. It was her equivalent to Patrick Leigh Fermor's *A Time to Keep Silence*. He used to stay in monasteries the same way. In fact, when her book came out, I put it on display alongside PLF's, not long before she died."

His mouth twisted in embarrassment as he realised what he'd just said.

"You mean this is a death threat?" I croaked. "But why?"

"I can't imagine, sweetheart. But I tell you what, we will think about it more clearly when we get out of the flat and into the fresh air. Finish your drink, I'll grab the picnic basket, and we'll be off."

12 Along the Way

Hand in hand, we strolled down the High Street to the junction with the Cotswold Way, the historic footpath that runs from Cheltenham to Bath, hugging the green and gentle contours of the hills. Each of us sunk in contemplation, we barely spoke until we'd walked for a few minutes along the dusty track, leaving the village behind us. The path slowly rose to yield a stunning view across the farmland below us.

"I don't think I've ever even met a nun to speak to," I began, feeling guilty that this was presently higher up my list of concerns than the vanishing corpse. "Let alone upset one enough for her to send me a threatening letter, and I can't imagine Auntie May would have done either. There was a monastery on the Greek island where the writing retreat was, but I never met any of its monks. Although I'd have liked to. There are plenty of questions I'd ask one, given the opportunity."

Hector pointed to a lush grassy knoll to the right of the path.

"Shall we stop here for our picnic? Have you walked far enough?"

"Plenty in this heat, thanks."

He dropped my hand and set the picnic basket gently on the ground. I sat down beside it, slipped off my sandals, and stretched out my legs, enjoying the slight movement of air at this elevation. Hector unfolded a sky-blue rug and spread it on the ground in front of us, before taking two ice packs off the top of a pile of intriguing tin foil parcels. I picked one up and held it to my chest, shivering with delight at its cooling effect through the thin cotton of my dress.

"If this nun knew where May lived, she'd only have to ask at the village shop or The Bluebird to find out who you are and what your name is," suggested Hector. "Although I suspect both Carol and Donald would be more familiar with Blue Nun than actual nuns."

"It's reasonable for a nun to know that May had died, too," I considered. "Quite apart from her gravestone in the village churchyard, some of the national papers ran her obituary."

Hector began laying out the foil packages on the picnic rug.

"I hope you're hungry, sweetheart."

"I don't know. I don't have much appetite in this heat to start with, quite apart from all the upset at the school, and now this strange letter. What is there?"

He surveyed the packages as if rising to a challenging memory test.

"There's cold chicken, cold sausages, ham sandwiches, tomatoes, cucumber, carrot sticks, crisps, and sausage rolls, then strawberries, shortbread, dark chocolate buttons, and peppermint creams."

"Goodness, I shall have to call you Ratty!"

He sat back on his heels and grinned.

"Only if I can call you Mole. *The Wind in the Willows* has the best picnic scene in English literature."

As he opened the parcel of chicken drumsticks, an aroma of zesty lemon and floral herbs rose up, reminding me of the delicious and fragrant meals I'd had in Greece. Suddenly realising I was very hungry indeed, I decided I could manage one after all.

"Anyway, sweetheart, when this nun says you're next, perhaps she's not being threatening. She might just mean you're next in line to become a successful author. Maybe she's a big fan of May Sayers's books who's got wind of your writing ambitions and wants to wish you well."

He took a chicken drumstick for himself and bit into it.

"Writing plans, Hector, and actions. Not just idle dreams as they were before I moved here. Goodness, what a difference a year makes." I smiled. What adifference Hector had made to my life, too. "Anyway, how would she know about that? I've only been published in the *Wendlebury Parish News* so far, and that little book you did for the Wendlebury Writers at Christmas. She's not to know I'm five chapters into my first novel."

He licked his lips.

"Maybe she's a writer too and saw your name announced in that writing magazine when you won the free place on the Greek trip."

I reached for a slice of red pepper, crisp and refreshing in the still heavy heat.

"It doesn't strike me as the sort of magazine a nun might read. Though I can't think which magazines nuns would prefer. All the same, I appreciate you trying to stop me worrying, Hector, but don't you think that if the nun wanted to encourage me, she would have at least signed the note with her name? Even if she used the name she adopted when she took her vows, rather than birth name. As it stands, it looks plain shifty."

"Maybe she belongs to a silent order so doesn't want you to reply. I think monks and nuns suppress their individuality, so she wouldn't be in search of a pen-friend exactly." Hector offered me the sausages, thick Gloucester Old Spot specials that I recognised from the village shop. "By the way, did you know that Trappist monks are allowed to speak to animals, but not to each other? While they are on farm duties, anyway. I read that in Patrick Leigh Fermor's book."

I chose the most appetising sausage, well browned on all sides.

"Hector, when you get fan letters for your books, do the senders sign their names?"

"It would be odd not to. Although they write to Hermione Minty, rather than to Hector Munro, of course, and they can only contact me via a form on my website." Hermione Minty was Hector's pen name. "I don't give out a postal address, or even an email address."

I was getting curious now.

"What sort of things do fans write to you about? Do they ask for signed photos?"

He laughed.

"They'd get a shock if I sent them one. Sometimes they say how much my books have helped them by providing escapism, inspiring them to resolve their romantic dilemmas, or even to write their own books. I've never had one from a nun, though, so you're ahead of me in that particular niche market."

No matter how much he said it, I still couldn't believe this strange note was fan mail. Did any nuns read the *Wendlebury Parish News*? I made a mental note to ask the vicar next time I saw him.

"Is there someone with the surname Nun and the initial A in the village?" I asked. "Arthur or Alison Nun, maybe?"

Hector shook his head. "Not to my knowledge.

"OK, enough about nuns. We mustn't let this phantom letter-writer distract us from the more pressing crisis of the day: Ella's disappearing dead body. I wanted to search the school, but she wouldn't let me."

As I helped myself to another chicken leg, Hector poured us each some sparkling apple juice. When I held it up to the light, it glowed like a sunset in a glass.

"No point searching for an invisible man. Besides, in the unlikely event that it is not just Ella's imaginary friend, in the current heatwave, a dead body will soon make its presence felt if it is lurking about the school somewhere." He pinched his nose closed. "Its fragrance will find you, and I'm not talking about after-shave."

I nearly choked on my apple juice.

"Ugh, what an awful thought! Anyway, it may not have been visible when you went to the lost property cupboard, but it was very visible to me. And touchable, if that's a word. I touched its hand and it was the coldest thing I've felt all day. It felt – it felt like –" I looked down. "It felt just like this chicken leg."

In a wave of revulsion, I squealed and hurled the drumstick as far as I could. A deeper answering squeal, like a delayed echo, startled us both. A moment later, the sound of dusty footsteps came trudging up the track that lay below us. Clutching the chicken leg, which now had a bite taken out of it, came Tommy Crowe, beaming as he saw us.

"Howzat for a catch?" he said with his mouth full. "How did you know I was there?"

I was glad the drumstick hadn't landed on the ground before he'd bitten into it.

"I didn't," I replied.

"Good. I was meant to be camouflaged."

"But your T-shirt is bright purple," said Hector. "How does that work?"

Tommy pointed to his stone-coloured cut-offs. "See? My bottom half blends in with the drystone walls. If I stand in front of one, people might think I'm standing behind it."

"And the purpose of that is?" enquired Hector.

I offered Tommy the cherry tomatoes to go with his chicken. He took a handful and slipped them into the pocket of his shorts.

"It's something to do," said Tommy. "School holidays are so boring." Uninvited, he dropped to his knees between us and the view, eyeing the spread on the rug.

"Tuck in, Tommy," said Hector, with a sigh. As a growing teenager, Tommy is always running on empty. "There's more than enough here for me and Sophie."

Tommy brightened. "Cheers, Hector. Have you got another glass? Being camouflaged is thirsty work."

"Sorry, Tommy, I wasn't expecting company."

Tommy waved his chicken-free hand airily. "No problem. I don't mind drinking from the bottle."

Before either of us could stop him, he had taken a hearty swig of apple juice. I resigned myself to not having any more to drink until we got back to Hector's flat.

"What you need is a project, Tommy," I said, ignoring his subsequent belch. "Like building a den or a fort or a coracle, something that will take you a while and that you can enjoy using for the rest of the summer."

Hector took a ham sandwich. "Or, as you're into camouflage, how about a hide?"

"What, you mean like hide and seek? That's a kids' game." Only a few months before, Tommy had been happily playing hide and seek with his little sister Sina in the churchyard. He was several inches taller now than he had been then.

Hector shook his head while finishing his mouthful of sandwich.

"No, I mean a birdwatchers' hide. It's a secret hiding place, covered in branches and foliage, with a tiny window like a letterbox. You can go inside and keep an eye on things outside, while the birds just think it's part of the landscape."

Tommy's eyes widened.

"That sounds brilliant! Where do you think I should put it?"

Hector raised his hands in protest.

"It's not for me to say, Tommy, or I'll be able to spot you when no-one else can." He shot me a conspiratorial look.

"Hector's right, Tommy. It's a place only you should know about. Build it somewhere really unlikely, where no-one would ever expect to see you. Otherwise it would just be a common or garden den."

Tommy wrinkled his nose. "Yes, dens are for babies."

For a moment, I wondered whether he was getting mixed up with playpens, but I didn't want to distract him by enquiring.

He dropped his stripped drumstick bone on the rug. Taking a sausage roll in one hand and a ham sandwich in the other, he got to his feet.

"Just to keep me going on the journey," he observed, waving them in case we hadn't noticed.

Hector suppressed a smile.

"Fair enough."

Reenergised, Tommy strode back up the Cotswold Way towards the village.

I turned to Hector.

"I wonder whether we'll spot him on our way back?"

Hector grinned.

"If we do, let's pretend not to see him. If we're lucky, Tommy being camouflaged will keep him out of our hair for the rest of the holidays."

From a plastic tub, he offered me strawberries, which proved to be at the peak of ripeness. The first one I took filled my whole mouth with flavour. Helping myself from a tin of shortbread triangles – petticoat tails, as we call them at home in Inverness – I layered a few strawberries on top, before adding a second triangle and squashing it down to release the juices. I held it for a few moments to allow the bottom piece of shortbread to absorb the pink liquid.

"But back to my body –" I began. Hector raised his eyes suggestively. "The dead body, I mean. Maybe whoever sent me that nasty note is involved with that somehow. Maybe they know Ella and I saw the body, and they're trying to intimidate me into silence."

Hector was watching the strawberry juice trickle down my wrist. I leaned forward to lick it up before biting the pointy end of the shortbread.

"Well, you know what to do with bullies," he said. "You either stand up to them or ignore them. And in this case, in the absence of an actual person to stand up to, ignoring them is the only option."

"That's all very well for you to say when you're not on the receiving end –" I began, but then my shortbread began to disintegrate, so I stopped talking to eat it.

Hector lay back on the grassy slope and clasped his hands behind his head.

"Anyway, what makes you think the note had anything to do with this phantom body?" He gazed up at the clear blue sky, the horizon now tinged with a rose blush.

"What do you mean, phantom? Why won't you believe me?"

I lay back beside him, clasping my hands across my stomach. Hector pointed up to a small plump cloud drifting above us.

"Tell me, Sophie, what does that cloud look like to you?"

The cloud was completely asymmetrical. On the left-hand side was a series of soft scallops, while down the right-hand side was a smooth curve, a jutting ridge, and a slight indentation.

"A face. It's definitely a face. A woman, judging by the hairstyle. Quite an elderly one, as she's got a perm. No one under seventy has a perm these days. Delicate feminine nose. Probably a nice person."

Hector lowered his hand and reached across to clasp mine.

"You know it's a cloud, right?"

I laughed. "Yes, obviously it's a cloud. I'm not thinking it's a giant severed head floating above us. Actually it reminds me of one of those big dummies you see in Lenten carnivals in Catholic countries, or a balloon person from a New York City parade."

He raised my hand to his lips and kissed it.

"Actually, it's pareidolia."

"Parry what now?"

He licked one of my fingertips. "Mmm, strawberry flavour. Pareidolia. The incorrect perception of a stimulus. Mistaking something for something else, seeing connections where there are none. It's the natural response of the human brain trying to make sense of its surroundings and interpreting them in a meaningful way. There's a touching short story by H G Wells called *The Presence by the Fire*, in which a newly bereaved widower finds comfort from his wife's ghostly presence as he sits by his fireside of an evening. Later he realises that the shape is not his wife, but only a chance pattern of shadows, cast by the firelight around a particular arrangement of furniture, that he interprets as her profile. So it is with clouds. We don't look at clouds and see a vast mass of water vapour particles; we see faces or running dogs or maps of Italy or whatever.

"You don't need the deductive powers of Sherlock Holmes to see what I'm driving at. Picture now your encounter in the lost property cupboard this morning. A pair of trainers becomes a body's feet, a discarded hoodie his torso, an abandoned rubber glove his chicken-leg fingers."

I pulled my hand away from his and turned onto my side to face him, propping myself up on one elbow.

"Do you know what I see when I look at you?" With my free hand, I brushed a stray curl back from his forehead. "An unspeakable cynic."

I wanted so badly to believe him, but my instincts were telling me he'd got it all wrong.

13 Where's the Fire?

The sun was low over the Welsh hills before we finally gathered up our picnic things and packed them back into Hector's basket. He'd just buckled the straps when I stood up and realised I'd been sitting on a piece of foil, then we almost forgot to pick up the rug.

By the time we got back to his flat, feeling sun-kissed and full, we were in philosophical mood. I was glad we hadn't yet fallen out over our differing interpretations of the day's events.

"There's the rest of your Vinho Verde in the fridge, if you'd like some," he said, fetching two wine glasses from the cupboard.

After throwing open the sash window of his sitting room, I noticed hanging over the fireside chair that I always think of as mine a pale pink cropped cardigan. I picked it up and shook out the creases. Hector set the bottle and glasses on the coffee table between the armchairs.

"That's funny, I don't remember you wearing that cardigan when you arrived, although it does look strangely familiar."

I stared at it for a moment. "That's because it isn't mine. But you know who it does belong to?"

Hector was filling the glass nearest me.

"No, who?"

"Your Anastasia, that's who."

Hector's aim slipped and he splashed a little wine onto the coffee table.

"In fact, she was wearing this when she came up here this afternoon," I went on. "What's she doing, lounging about and disrobing in my armchair?"

Hector pulled a tissue from the box to wipe up the spillage.

"She was probably just too hot," he said evenly. He took another tissue to wipe his brow as if to prove his point, although his forehead was as dry as a cream cracker.

I was having none of it.

"Besides, I thought she was only meant to be working in your book room, not having free rein of the flat?"

I glanced in the direction of the spare room that housed his curiosities collection, half-expecting Anastasia to appear in the doorway with a cheery cry of "Surprise!" Hector filled his own glass and took a long swig without looking at me.

"Sophie, you're being absurd. You'll be telling me next that this flat isn't big enough for the three of us."

I wished I'd thought of that line.

He raised his glass to me.

"Come on, now, we've had a lovely evening getting away from it all. Let's not spoil it."

I frowned.

"But don't you find it odd that Anastasia was apparently loitering around the village for a couple of hours this morning just when the dead body was coming and going?"

Hector covered his eyes.

"Oh, come off it. She's a tiny little thing; she could no more haul a dead body about the place than I could lift my Land Rover."

He had a point. Such petty jealousy was unbecoming. After all, it had been my idea to catalogue his curiosities collection to sell online. I decided to change the subject and glanced at my watch.

"I'll just phone Ella before we go to bed to check she's OK."

Hector brightened. "Now that's a good idea." I didn't think he was referring to phoning Ella.

I gazed at the screen of my mobile as it rang out.

"She's not answering her phone."

"Perhaps she's in bed already," said Hector.

"It's not even dark yet."

"Still, she had a tiring day. Hysteria can be very wearing."

I was too worried to rise to that bait.

"I'm not going to bed till I've spoken to her. I won't sleep unless I know she's OK."

"Who said anything about sleeping?" murmured Hector, draining the bottle into our glasses. But he needn't have worried. Hardly had he put the bottle down when my phone rang, and Ella's name flashed up on the screen.

"Ella, thank goodness!" I settled back into my armchair. "Are you OK?"

"Sophie, I'm fine, honest. The afternoon off hit the spot. But are you OK?"

"Yes, I'm fine. I'm at Hector's. Although —" I hesitated, unsure whether to trouble her about my threatening letter. "No, I'm fine. All OK at your flat?"

At least if she'd received a similar missive, this would give her the chance to tell me about it.

"Mmm." She sounded distracted.

"Did your mum come round? Ian said you might call her."

She laughed.

"Yes, that's what I told Ian, bless him. No, I wouldn't want to worry Mum. But —" she lowered her voice, "— I'm finding Ash a real comfort."

"Ash? What are you talking about?" Surely she hadn't found the body and somehow managed to cremate it to hide the evidence? I knew she wanted to protect the school's reputation, but burning a mysterious corpse would bring even more ill-repute.

She was whispering now. "Ash. My new boyfriend. Haven't I told you about him? He's a fireman and, believe me, he really knows how to comfort a girl in a crisis, if you get my drift."

I burst out laughing, much to Hector's surprise.

"Ash is a fireman? Surely that's not his real name?"

"Yes, short for Ashad. Haven't you heard that name before? It's not unusual. Not as unusual as Anastasia. That's Greek, isn't it? Or is it Russian?"

"I don't know," I said testily, annoyed at her for reminding me of Anastasia. But her words prompted me to recall sitting next to a Greek woman called Anastasia on the plane home from my retreat. We'd had a very long chat, and she'd turned out to be a fan of Auntie May's books. When I told her my name was Sophie, she had asked me whether I was Greek, despite my light brown hair. It crossed my mind to wonder whether that other

Anastasia could have been a nun on holiday, in plain clothes rather than a habit.

"Yes, of course I have. It just struck me as a funny name for a fireman. Sorry, Ella. Sorry, Ash." I called the latter louder in case he could hear me. But Ella clearly wasn't in the mood for a long conversation, and soon made her excuses and hung up.

When I regaled Hector about Ella's latest attachment, he was equally amused. "I hope no-one's told him that with Ella, he's likely to be an old flame sooner rather than later. Do you think he'll give her a fireman's lift to the bedroom?"

I drained my glass and set it gently on the table. Those glasses are delicate, left over from when Hector's House was his parents' antiques shop.

"No pressure, Hector." I grinned. "I can make my own way to yours."

***

Not long after 2am, I awoke with a start and had to think for a moment why my bed had a different view from usual. Then I remembered I was at Hector's, and the events of the previous day began racing through my mind. How much had I really imagined? Hector's explanation of the permed cloud had made me doubt my own eyes.

Restless, I wriggled out from beneath the thin summer duvet and padded as quietly as I could to the kitchen to fetch a glass of water. Rather than risk waking Hector by opening a cupboard door for a fresh glass, I picked an empty tumbler up from the counter. As I held it under the tap, a shaft of moonlight streamed in through the small kitchen window, catching the delicate pattern etched under the rim – and a distinct half-kiss shape in pale pearly lipstick.

I jumped so much that I nearly dropped the tumbler. Steadying myself on the chilly porcelain, I flung the contents of the glass into the sink with as much revulsion as if it had been poison and stalked back to bed, my mouth dry.

14 Normal Service Is Resumed

Over breakfast, Hector told me more about his plans for Anastasia.

"As there's no computer in my flat, she's kindly bringing her own laptop and will piggyback off the shop's wifi to log into our website's backend."

Slicing the strawberries left over from our picnic into my bowl of vanilla yoghurt, I didn't care about the technological details.

"So does that mean she'll be in the flat in your book room all day?"

He snaffled the last whole strawberry from the chopping board.

"Well, yes, apart from when we need her in the shop. I'll give her some initial training, too. That's only reasonable." Hector is annoyingly reasonable. "Besides, you were glad enough of her help in the tearoom yesterday when you were faffing about at the school with Ella."

Not so reasonable.

"Just so I know, when she's up here –" I tried to sound casual, "– she is meant to stick to the book room, isn't she? I'd hate to give her misinformation."

He got up from the breakfast bar to collect a muffin from the toaster.

"Of course. It's not like I've asked her to clean the flat in her idle moments. Of which there shouldn't be any, until she's catalogued every single book."

I stirred the strawberry slices around in my bowl, making fragrant scarlet swirls against the ivory yoghurt.

"How will she know how to price them?"

Perching on the stool beside me, he began to spread glistening butter the colour of cowslips over his lightly toasted muffins. The day was going to be another scorcher if the butter was melting already.

"She won't. I'll estimate the prices from the data she inputs. She will just do background research, looking each title up on other sites, noting the prices charged for the same book in the same condition. She'll also record any points of difference such as autographs. Personal inscriptions can make a real difference to the price of a collectible. Once she's finished inputting all the data, I'll review each record and add the prices."

I slid a generous spoonful of yoghurt and strawberries into my mouth, savouring the blend of acid and sweetness.

"Any idea how many books you've got in there?"

I was wondering how long it would take Anastasia to complete the project.

Hector took a bite of muffin to buy thinking time, gazing into the distance as he tried to work it out in his head. Giving up, he reached across the counter for his shopping list and jotted some figures down: 3 x 7 x 3 x 20…

"A few thousand, I suppose," he said once his mouth was empty. "Goodness, I didn't realise I had so many. So if we sell fifty a week, even at a modest average of a fiver each, assuming we charge the customer postage and packing, we could gross a thousand pounds a month. Not bad when you consider most of those books cost me no more than a pound each at jumble sales and car boot sales. We could do a lot with an extra grand in our monthly budget."

Was it mean of me to be glad that a grand wouldn't cover the cost of an extra salary?

Hector stared out of the window at the cloudless bluebell sky.

"I'm glad you said 'we'," I said quietly. That broke his daydream.

"Why? Are you after a pay rise?"

"No, I just like to think of us being in this venture together."

He patted my shoulder. "Well, the curiosities shop was your idea."

I was feeling more cheerful until Anastasia tripped into the shop later that morning, bright as a kitten. I'd slipped her cardigan into my bag without mentioning it to Hector. Once we opened up the shop, I'd draped it over the back of the tearoom chair closest to the front door. Anastasia couldn't fail to spot its sugar-pink glow as she reported for work.

"Morning, Hector. Morning, Sophie. Oh, great, there's my top, I thought I must have left it in the tearoom."

She all but skipped over to retrieve it. I started wiping the nearest table as an excuse to talk to her out of Hector's hearing.

"I found it in Hector's flat, actually, on one of his fireside chairs."

She beamed, stuffing the cardigan into her bubblegum-pink backpack.

"They're very comfy, those chairs, and so delicious in this heat, cold leather against bare skin. You should try them."

I was speechless. Had Hector not told her that he and I are in a relationship? I decided not to mention the tumbler stained with lipstick, an exact match to the pale pearly shade of her lips right now.

A moment later, she was behind the trade counter, standing too close to Hector as he finished gift-wrapping a blank journal for Mrs Fortescue, the chair of the WI.

"OK, boss, so is now a good time for my training?"

He glanced at his watch, then around the shop. All the customers were seated in the tearoom or quietly browsing the stock.

"Yes, that's fine. Pull up a chair from the tearoom, and I'll show you the structure of the stock database and how to input to it."

"Oh, I don't need a chair. I've been sitting down on the bus all the way here, and I could do with a stretch."

As if to demonstrate, she raised her arms above her head. The hem of her short denim skirt edged up a couple of centimetres.

At that moment, in strolled Billy. His face lit up at the sight of Anastasia in mid-stretch.

"Aye aye, what's this? Physical jerks in the bookshop of a morning? Have you taken up those aerobicals, Hector? Is this a new get-fit scheme you're running for your customers?"

He stopped by the counter to wag a finger at Anastasia.

"You can count me out, girlie. My sporting days are long gone." He tapped his left knee, lurking somewhere in the depths of his baggy corduroy trousers. "See this

89

knee? I sprained it celebrating last time the England football team won the World Cup."

Anastasia looked puzzled.

"I didn't know England had ever won the World Cup."

Billy tutted.

"Don't they teach you nothing useful at school these days? In 1966 against Germany."

Anastasia's eyes widened.

"That's before my dad was born."

Hector chipped in before Billy could reply.

"Billy, Anastasia is our new intern for the summer holidays. I'm just going to train her on our stock system, then she'll be off upstairs to catalogue my curiosities collection."

Billy lifted his cap to scratch his head. "I shall have to call you Annie. I can't get my dentures round a foreign name like that."

At least he's calling her by her name, I thought bitterly. I should never have let him get away with calling me 'girlie' the first time we met. No wonder Hector still looks on my role in the shop as lowly.

"Morning, Sophie, love," Billy added, as if to prove me wrong.

While Billy settled down at his favourite tearoom table, I prepared his morning coffee and brought it over. Having served all the other tearoom customers, I took a seat beside Billy for a catch-up. Living alone, he comes to Hector's House more for the social side than sustenance.

He jerked his head in the direction of the trade counter, where Anastasia was now leaning forward to peer at Hector's screen. Her long, crinkly dark curls, whether natural or the legacy of the previous day's fishtail plait, tumbled towards his lap.

"That young Annie's dressed more like a magician's sidekick than a bookshop assistant."

I didn't like to ask what he thought I looked like.

Anastasia peeled off a turquoise wrap top to reveal a tangerine vest with spaghetti straps. When I'd selected my Indian frock from May's wardrobe the previous evening, I'd thought it was an appetising mix of spicy shades, but now I felt like a thrush beside a kingfisher. Anastasia was at least two dress sizes smaller than me, too.

"It doesn't really matter what she wears as most of the time she'll be working up in Hector's curiosities room, out of the public eye."

Billy stirred his coffee and licked the foam from his teaspoon.

"How old is she again?" he asked with a sniff.

"Eighteen. She's just left school."

"By the time my old mum was eighteen, she'd been out of school six years, married for two and I was one." He leaned towards me and lowered his voice. "You got any of those security cameras upstairs?"

He pointed at our only camera, mounted on the wall at the back of the shop. It was actually an old biscuit tin, strategically painted, but Hector hoped it might have a deterrent effect, as it could be seen from the front door and the trade counter.

"No, but I think that's a very good idea, Billy. For Anastasia's safety, I mean." An inspired touch. "We can't have a young girl working alone in Hector's flat unsupervised, just in case a stranger wanders up there."

"How about one of them remote control babby things?"

"Remote controlled babies? Whatever do you mean?"

"You know, one of those things that lets you hear babbies crying in a different room. Reason I'm asking is that I just saw one advertised on the noticeboard in the village shop. Someone is selling one for a tenner. It might serve you a turn."

"Oh, a baby monitor. I see. Great idea, Billy." I smiled sweetly. "Why don't you suggest it to Hector on your way out?"

15 The Fireman's Lift

After the busy lunch period, Hector asked me whether I'd like to go back up to the school to finish organising the library. I think he was working on the principle of getting back on a bicycle straight after falling off.

"In the unlikely event of a coach party arriving when you're not here, I can always call Anastasia down to help," he said cheerfully.

Although I was nervous of returning to the school, I could feel the afternoon sunshine doing me good as I strolled up the High Street, breathing fresh air instead of tearoom steam. As I approached the school's front door, I was glad to see that Ella had her office window wide open and the only music issuing forth was a soothing new-age harp track.

I punched in the code to open the front door, 1314, remembering my last trip to the Battle of Bannockburn Visitor Centre in Scotland. I hoped one day I'd be able to take Hector there.

Once inside the entrance hall, I knocked on Ella's office door.

"Come in!" Her voice was bright and strong, which boded well for her state of mind.

I made myself comfortable in her visitor's chair as she fired up her coffee machine. This time she handed me a Best Teacher mug.

"So did you have a fun picnic last night with your Hector?"

I appreciated the 'your'. I needed that reassurance.

"Yes, thanks. And how's your fireman?"

She beamed. "Just the emergency service I needed. He made me feel so much better about the events of yesterday. Much more than my mum could have done."

"I assume their techniques are rather different."

She put her hands on her hips.

"Actually, we had a very sensible discussion and he put my mind at rest. He sees things like this all the time at fire call-outs."

"What, disappearing dead bodies?"

"No, silly, mass hysteria. People imagining things, especially when they're under stress. One person gets anxious and passes it on to the next, and before you know it, everyone's upset."

I frowned.

"But that's not how it happened. I got upset quite independently, before I knew that you'd seen the body too. Besides, two people don't count as a mass. Two's company, not a crowd."

"No, but you know what I mean. We get it here in school, where one child throws up, and if you don't deal with it pronto, before you know it, half the class have their heads in buckets."

"Or when one of them decides on a school trip that they get travel sick or need a wee."

Ella nodded. "Or like nuns synchronising their monthly cycles in a convent."

I sat up straight.

"Nuns? What do you know about nuns?"

She waved a hand, languid in the afternoon heat. "Apart from that, nothing. That is the sum total of my knowledge about nuns."

I decided to let it go. I didn't want to tell her about my threatening letter just yet.

"Actually, Ella, I think Ash and Hector are more alike than you realise. Hector was also going on about the power of suggestion last night, only he had a fancy name for it. For seeing animate objects in inanimate things."

"What, you mean like seeing the face of Benedict Cumberbatch in your cappuccino foam?"

I nodded. "It made sense the way he explained it, and I can see where he's coming from."

Suddenly, Ella fixed her eyes on me.

"Actually, Sophie, neither of us believes Ash or Hector, do we? Not really?"

"I know. I'm still convinced I saw an actual dead body. Although Hector also has a theory about it being a live one. He thinks the workmen might have been playing a practical joke on us, or that one of them was concussed and went into the lost property cupboard to lie down and recover."

"Why not just lie down on the field in the fresh air? Or in their van if they wanted privacy?"

"Exactly!" I wished I'd thought of saying that to Hector. "Besides, neither of us is prone to hysteria. Why would we imagine something so unlikely?"

"And why would I make up a dead body that looked so much like my ex-boyfriend? That would be incriminating myself."

I considered for a moment. "And was this Lawrence Byrne the type to play dead as a practical joke? I mean, in the very unlikely event that the mystery man might actually be your friend Lawrence."

"Not at all. He was very serious, and besides, he had no imagination. He couldn't have faked a thing. I don't really think it could have been him."

"How did you meet him?"

And what did you see in him? I wanted to ask, but didn't.

"Through a dating website for teachers."

"But you're not a teacher."

"No, I know. But I was fed up with dating men who don't understand what it is like to work in a school. You won't believe the number of men who assume that you get all the school holidays off and finish work at three o'clock every day. Often I'd be working longer hours than they did. Whereas firemen are so used to working antisocial shifts that they're grateful for any time you're off work."

I gazed into my coffee mug.

"There's another issue we haven't resolved yet. When we tried to prepare a description for the police after the body disappeared, we couldn't agree on the details, even though we'd only seen it that morning."

She frowned.

"Yes, it was like we were describing two different people."

I looked up at her in alarm as a new idea occurred to me.

"Is it possible that we each in fact did see a different dead body?"

"You mean there were two different men in the cupboard at different times?"

I gulped.

"Exactly. And then there were none."

16 Kate Takes Charge

A sharp rap at the school's front door made us both jump, and I set down my mug on Ella's desk.

"Who are you expecting?" I asked, glancing at the wall clock.

Ella shrugged. "No-one. I've no appointments until tomorrow."

She came round from behind her desk and grabbed my hand to haul me out of my chair.

"Let's answer it together. Safety in numbers."

We trooped out to the entrance hall, and Ella opened the front door slowly.

"Ooh, a delegation!" cried Kate Blake, clapping her hands as she crossed the threshold. "I may be a school governor, but there's no need to stand on ceremony. Sorry to disturb you, but I got my battles mixed up for the door code. I was trying the Battle of Bosworth. I knew it began with a B. Anyway, I've just had coffee with Hector, and as I was walking back this way, I thought I'd call in to see how the workmen are getting on in the playground. May I go through?"

"Sure," said Ella.

Kate carried on, humming to herself, while Ella and I returned to her office.

"I bet she wasn't just walking by," Ella said in a low voice. "That wretched boyfriend of yours told her I was in a state and sent her to check up on me. Honestly, what a traitor. Blood may be thicker than water, but they're not even proper relatives. He's only her godson."

She gripped my arm so hard I feared she'd leave bruises. "If Kate gets the impression I can't cope with my responsibilities here, at this tiny school, I'll never get a promotion. I was planning to look for a job at a bigger school in the next couple of years, and I was going to ask Kate to be one of my referees."

"Let me leave you in peace, then, so it doesn't look like I'm wasting your time gossiping. While I'm finishing sorting out the library, I'll catalogue and shelve the new books I delivered yesterday, too."

I picked up the box of books that still lay unopened on her meeting table. Grabbing the paperknife from the wonky china pencil pot some child must have made for her, I slashed the sticky tape used to seal the box.

"My goodness, that's sharp!" I cried, wedging the blade safely among the pencils and pens in the clay pot. "Don't let the kids borrow it, or they'll turn the school into a crime scene."

Perhaps it already was.

***

An hour later, once I had the library shelves in pristine order, I took a stack of damaged books for repair to Ella's office and asked to borrow her sticky tape and scissors. Just as I was taping a ripped spine onto a Michael

Morpurgo, there came another knock, this time at Ella's office door.

"Come in, Kate," Ella called, a note of resignation in her voice.

The door immediately flew wide open. On the threshold stood not Kate, but Dai, the jokey one of the playground builders, now with a face fit to fell drystone walls.

He waved the hard hat in his hand.

"What do you think you're doing, telling that prying woman we haven't been wearing our hard hats?" he thundered.

Ella and I looked at each other in bewilderment.

"I didn't," she protested.

No, but I guessed Hector did. Hector knows Kate is governor responsible for health and safety, and if his concussion theory was right, it was fair game for him to report the workmen before anyone was seriously hurt.

"Well, she's been going flipping ape out there, threatening to report us to the council and get us blacklisted from working for schools. Is that the gratitude we get for doing this deal superfast at our lowest possible rate? After letting you sweet talk us into rescheduling our other jobs to fit you in?"

Ella was not easily cowed.

"Well, you aren't wearing your hard hats, are you?" she said tersely. "In fact, I haven't seen you wear them since you arrived on site."

Dai wasn't finished.

"It was bad enough to have that Hercule Poirot fellow snooping around yesterday. Is this how you work at this school, sending a different governor to check up on us each day? I thought you were the boss here, not just some ditsy, dopey girl who faints at the sight of a dead mouse and gets the grown-ups to do her dirty work."

That did it. Ella sprang from her chair and slammed her hands so hard onto the desk that it must have hurt. Dai took a step back.

"NEVER call me ditsy!" she roared. "And put your wretched hard hat on, now. I don't want you or your mates incurring head wounds on my watch, so don't tempt me to test just how hard your skull is without it."

For a moment, Dai stared open-mouthed. Rosy-cheeked, dark eyes gleaming, Ella was almost panting with rage. Dai put on his hat and backed towards the door, glancing awkwardly at me as if afraid I was about to gang up with Ella against him.

"OK, as long as we're clear on that, then," he said, before pulling the door closed. The scuffling of feet in the entrance hall revealed his mates had been listening to the confrontation.

"My God, she's even more sexy when she's angry," we heard Dai hiss. "Now, hats on, lads, and let's see if we can finish clearing the ground before the end of the day."

We waited until their footsteps had retreated beyond the French doors before falling about laughing.

Ella was first to recover.

"Well, I've got to keep them on track somehow. If the new playground's not finished by the start of next term, the PTA will go bananas, and I can't afford to fall out with the PTA. Nor with Kate and the rest of the governors. Honestly, sometimes I feel like a chess piece when most of the other pieces in my colour have been taken, the rest don't understand the rules, and the other side are advancing across the board in perfect formation."

I never knew she played chess.

Her office door creaked open again.

"Who's perfectly formed?" Kate materialised in the doorway, bright and breezy. "Ella, I've just had a nice chat with the workmen, and then a catch-up with dear Ian. Do you have five minutes to go through the plans for the health and safety meeting with me, please? Unless you're in the middle of something important with Sophie?"

When Kate flashed me her most winning smile, I gathered the books into my arms, with Ella's scissors and sticky tape balanced on the top.

"Don't mind me, I can finish my repairs in the library."

"I suppose you're in no rush to get back to the bookshop now Hector's got that lovely young girl helping him in the tearoom," said Kate.

"In the tearoom?" I dropped the books back on the table and Michael Morpurgo's spine fell off again. "Actually, Ella, I'll pop back tomorrow to finish my repairs, if you don't mind."

I was up the High Street faster than Dai had donned his hard hat.

17 Taking Over the Asylum

"He's gone upstairs to sort that Antistatic out," said Tommy, spinning round on Hector's stool behind the trade counter. "And he took a screwdriver with him."

"Why, what has she done?"

As I caught sight of the empty baby monitor packaging beside Hector's laptop, Tommy stopped spinning and put his hand over the box proprietorially.

"I did an errand for Hector. I came in to ask if he had any odd jobs he needed doing, and he asked me to go to the shop to get the phone number for the advert Billy told him about, and then he phoned it, and then I went to collect this for him and give the lady the money, and then he went upstairs, and now I'm in charge."

"Thanks, Tommy, that was helpful."

It's always worth catching Tommy doing something right. At my praise, he sat up a bit straighter, his knees scraping the counter. His spinning had raised the stool to its highest level. Immediately he set to work to spin himself back the other way. He reminded me of Alice in Wonderland, eating the right side and the left side of the mushroom to attain the perfect height.

"So who's manning the tearoom if Hector and Anastasia are upstairs? Or are you doing that as well?"

I glanced over to see Tommy's little sister, Sina, swamped beneath one of my aprons, sitting cross-legged on the tearoom counter and tucking into a chocolate chip cookie. Two middle-aged ladies at the only occupied table shot me a pleading look. I acknowledged them with a little wave.

"I'll be over to take your order in just a moment," I called.

By the time I looked back at Tommy, his chin was on the counter. He began to spin the other way.

"Hector said he wouldn't be long, but he has been," said Tommy. "I'd quite like to get back to building my hide now. Sina will stay and help you, though, won't you, Sina?"

"Just hang on for a minute while I nip up and get Hector," I said. "It can't take him that long to install a baby monitor."

"Are you going to have a baby, then, Sophie?"

Sina's clear, high voice ricocheted around the shop. Every customer's head turned towards me.

"No, I am not!" I wanted to quash that rumour before I headed for the door.

The downstairs door to Hector's flat stood wide open, saving me the need to ring the bell. I was glad about that. I didn't want to give Anastasia the impression that she had free access to his flat when I didn't.

When I reached the top of the stairs, they were sitting at the breakfast bar, calmly drinking iced coffee. I made a mental note that in this heatwave it would be a great idea to put iced coffee on the café menu. I'd drunk a lot of it during my week in Greece and had got quite hooked. I hoped Anastasia wouldn't realise that she'd given me the idea.

At the sound of my footsteps, Hector turned in my direction.

"Oh, hi, Sophie. Everything OK at the school?"

"Fine, thanks, but it's getting busy downstairs, so when you're ready –"

He got up from the stool, drained his mug, and licked his lips.

"Thanks for the *café frappé*, Anastasia, it was delicious."

That's what they'd called it in Greece.

But it's your coffee! And your milk! And your mugs! I wanted to shout, but Anastasia's sweet smile deterred me. Instead, I vented my frustration on Hector as I followed him down the stairs.

"What are you thinking, putting Tommy and Sina in charge of the shop? Whatever next? Shall I put Blossom on the payroll?"

Hector laughed, unperturbed even by the mention of his nemesis.

"Well, they were hanging around in the street outside, and it kept them out of mischief for a while. Not that I'm planning to make a habit of it."

Of what? Spending time upstairs with Anastasia? I couldn't eradicate from my mind the intimate scene of her perching on the stool where only hours ago I'd been eating my breakfast after spending the night with him.

Before we turned the corner, I grabbed his arm to delay his return to the shop. Interpreting my gesture as a show of affection, he covered my hand with his.

"Hector, did you tell Kate the playground workmen weren't wearing their hard hats?"

"Yes, and why not? If it's already caused one of those idiots to get a head injury, she needs to put a stop to it before anything more serious happens. Just think what a bad start it would give to the new playground if it put a grown man in hospital, or worse, before it even opened."

"The PTA would be furious," I conceded. "But did you know Kate went to tell the workmen off about it after she left you? Then they stormed in to see Ella and upset her. Long story short, I don't think they'll make that mistake again. But also —"

Out of the corner of my eye, I saw the two ladies who I'd promised to serve leaving the shop. Putting duty first, I ran towards them.

"I'm so sorry, ladies, I'm back now. What can I get you, tea or coffee? And will you take a free bun on the house to thank you for your patience?"

They looked at each other and giggled.

"Ooh, well, if you insist, though we shouldn't really," said one.

"That would be lovely," said the other. "Two Earl Greys with lemon, please."

As we followed them into the shop, Tommy, still manning the trade counter, was holding a bearded gentleman's ten-pound note up to the light.

"Och, it's perfectly valid, son," the man was telling him.

Recognising the precise enunciation, I gave him my best apologetic smile. "I'm so sorry, sir, you are absolutely right." Then I turned to Tommy. "It's a Scottish tenner, Tommy. It's just as valid here as in Scotland; it's all pounds sterling. You can take it as payment, no problem."

Tommy looked for reassurance to Hector, who had paused to straighten the books on the display table nearest the door.

"OK, but next time I do this, Hector had better tell me the Scottish exchange rate first."

Fortunately, our Scottish visitor found Tommy's ignorance funny rather than offensive. "One day soon, son, we'll have the Euro in Alba, and then you Sassenachs will be sorry."

He winked at me as he waited patiently for Tommy to pick up a pound and a penny change. I couldn't resist the opportunity for a bit of Scottish-themed chat. I hadn't been to see my parents in Inverness since Christmas, and I was missing Scotland as well as them.

"Am I right in thinking you hail from Aberdeen, sir?" I asked.

"I did specify Earl Grey, didn't I, Sophie?" called one of the ladies from the tearoom.

"Oh, yes, I'm sorry." I smiled at the Scottish gentleman. "Enjoy your stay and do come again."

"Aye, I'll do ma best, natives permitting. Good afternoon tae ye."

As I returned to the tearoom, my head was a jumble, and while I took over making the drinks and taking the money, I let Sina stay on as waitress to give myself space to think. The tearoom customers thought she was awfully cute in her outsize pinny, and their tips were enough to make me worry she'd be volunteering every day for the rest of the holidays.

Needing calm, I took the opportunity to clear out the drawers beneath the tearoom counter one at a time, wiping the insides before replacing the contents neatly, followed by the cupboards of plates, glasses, mugs and cutlery. Meanwhile, my mind was racing with fresh possibilities.

I once read about a law lecturer whose first lesson for new students was on the unreliability of evidence. During the lecture, while he was speaking about something else, a supposed criminal would dash across the front of the lecture hall, giving students only a few seconds to register what he looked like. Afterwards, the professor would ask them to describe the villain, and the students were horrified to discover each of them offered a completely different description. There, said the professor, remember throughout your career that eyewitness evidence should never be trusted.

To identify our dead body, we needed more than visual clues of dubious accuracy. To find the murderer, we needed motives.

Might Ash be the jealous type and have murdered Ella's ex? If anyone could move bodies around easily, a firefighter could. Or he might be over-controlling? He might have dumped Lawrence in the lost property cupboard to intimidate Ella into obeying him, then whisked his body away to who knew where. As Ash worked unsociable shifts, he could have been around that morning, sneaking into the school behind Ella. He could have hidden nearby and watched her punch in the door code, or looked it up on the sly in her diary or on her phone.

Ash would have his work cut out if he was going to eliminate all his past competition, though. He would put any future boyfriends right off, too. Maybe that was his intention.

Sina broke my reverie by dumping a full tray of dirty crockery on the counter.

"Hector says it's home-time, so I'll be off now, Sophie."

She turned round so I could untie the strings of her apron, which she took off and shook upside down to empty her tips out of the pocket. When a pound coin fell to the floor and rolled away, she scampered after it like a kitten with a ping-pong ball. Then Hector found her an empty bank bag, held it open while she filled it, and folded the top over to keep her money safe.

Sina beamed.

"Thanks, Hector. Thanks, Sophie. School summer holidays are the best."

She skipped over to the door just as Tommy was walking in. Quick as a flash, she flipped the door sign round.

"Sorry, sir, we're closed!" she cried gleefully, before pushing past him and running off towards the village shop.

18 Don't Shoot the Messenger

"Special delivery for Mr House!"

Undeterred by the "closed" sign, Tommy waved a small white envelope bearing a single line of handwritten text.

"Mr Munro to you." Hector strolled over to collect his letter. "What, no stamp? Nor is there any address. Is it from you, Tommy? You can just talk to me, you know. No need to stand on ceremony."

Tommy glanced at the doormat beneath his feet, before patting the fraying fisherman's satchel slung over his shoulder.

"It's not from me, Hector, I'm just the postman."

"That's news to me. What about Raymond?"

Raymond, the local postman, toured the village around lunchtime every day, dispensing mail and cheery greetings.

"Of course there's Raymond. There's always been Raymond. No, what I'm offering is a personal mail service, for Wendlebury Barrow only. Didn't you see my special postbox?"

Hector looked him up and down.

"No, where are you hiding it? Is it in that old bag?"

"No, it's outside the village shop. Carol told me I could put it there."

"Oh, so that's what that big green box is." I came out from behind the tearoom counter to start cleaning the tables and chairs. "The one with a pair of wings painted on the side. I thought it was storage for Carol's stock of wild birdseed."

Tommy's face fell.

"But that's my postal service logo. The wings are to show how fast I deliver it. Same day service. Didn't you notice it says WILD underneath? That's short for Wendlebury Instant Letter Delivery. I'm much quicker than the Post Office."

I wrinkled my nose.

"Sorry, Tommy, I think you'd better put some instructions on the box to make its purpose clear."

Tommy stuffed his hands into the pockets of his khaki shorts and scuffed his shoes on the doormat.

"No wonder not many people are using it."

Poor Tommy. He's a natural entrepreneur, he just needs to fine-tune his ideas.

"You'd better put a note of your prices on your post box, if you're going to make any money out of it," advised Hector. "Where can people buy your stamps? I see there's no stamp on my letter."

Hector frowned as he looked at it again.

Tommy leaned against the doorway, as if feeling the weight of this interrogation.

"No, I haven't quite worked out how to do that yet."

Anticipating a request that we might start selling Tommy's stamps at Hector's House, I intervened.

"I've got a better idea. In the olden days, before stamps were invented, it wasn't the sender who paid for the postage, but the recipient. It might make life easier if

110

you did it that way round. Then anyone could post a letter in your box without needing to buy a stamp, and you just ask the person to whom you deliver each letter to pay a fee, say 50p."

Tommy brightened.

"Thanks, Sophie, great idea." He pulled his hands from his pockets and held one out to Hector. "That'll be 50p, please, Hector."

I burst out laughing. "Go on, Hector, cough up!"

Hector slumped down onto his stool, now restored to its usual height, opened the till and fished out a 50p piece.

"Whatever's in here had better be worth the money," he said as he handed the coin to Tommy.

Seeing Tommy's face fall, I came to his defence.

"Oh, Hector, don't be such a spoilsport. It's a good idea in principle. Well done, Tommy, I'm impressed by your entrepreneurial spirit."

Tommy's frown deepened.

"Is that like methylated spirit? I think we've got some of that in our garden shed."

Without waiting for an answer, he loped over to me and held out his hand. "I delivered a letter to your cottage yesterday, Sophie, so can I have 50p from you, too, please?"

So it was Tommy who had delivered my threatening letter. I wondered whether Carol had seen the nun as she dropped it in his postbox. Delving behind the tearoom counter for my handbag, I fished some 10p and 5p coins out of my purse.

"Thanks, Sophie. See, Hector, that's a pound I've made already today. You might want to try this idea yourself once I go back to school in September. I won't have time to do stuff like this then. I only see it as a holiday job. I'll sell you my green box, if you like."

111

"Thank you, Tommy, I'll bear that in mind. Now, as your sister rightly advised, the shop is closed. Home-time!"

"OK, see you guys tomorrow!"

With a friendly wave, Tommy bounded away.

Hector closed the door and leaned against it, one hand over his face.

"One day that boy will go far," I declared.

"Wherever he goes, it won't be far enough." Hector returned to the trade counter to cash up.

I tossed my cleaning cloth into the sink before going to join Hector at the trade counter, where he'd left Tommy's letter. As soon as I caught sight of the handwriting on the envelope, a chill ran through me.

"Hang on, Hector, that's the same scrawl as on the letter I got yesterday. Don't you recognise it?"

I sensed that he did but was trying to play it down so as not to worry me. He just continued cashing up.

Impatient, I seized his letter opener, slit the top of the envelope and shook the contents onto his desk. Just like mine, it was a small single unfolded sheet, written in the same uncertain hand.

I read it aloud. "I know your secret. Do you know it's illegal? From A Nun."

Hector stopped counting pound coins.

"My secret? She can't mean my pen-name. There's nothing illegal about a pseudonym. There's only one thing she can mean: selling my special cream."

"I thought monks and nuns liked alcohol? Aren't they famous for their beer and liqueurs?"

Hector shrugged. "Yes, you're right. Chartreuse liqueur, Trappist beer. But the difference is, they do it commercially with a licence to sell."

My smile at the notion of Trappist beer soon faded.

"You have to admit, Hector, that you have been playing with fire. Serving up illegal hooch in a cream jug does smack of the Prohibition. Have you ever seen the film *Some Like It Hot*?" He nodded, smiling at the recollection. "Remember the scene in which a nightclub is raided by the police and a drunken customer stumbles out onto the street, saying, 'I want another cup of coffee'?"

As Hector stared at the note in silence, I continued.

"I confess I have a certain affection for your cream, not only because it's delicious, but because when you spiked my drink at my job interview, it gave me the confidence to really go for it. But frankly, looking back now, I find it morally reprehensible, never mind illegal. What if you got caught? Did you know there's no ceiling on the financial penalties for selling illegal alcohol? How can it be worth risking the business that you've worked so hard to develop?"

Hector folded his arms on the counter and sank his head onto them.

"OK, I get the message. You're absolutely right, of course. To be honest, it all started out as a bit of fun when I was running the shop on my own, and it did help me attract regulars like Billy. Plus it's pure profit. Since I got the still up and running, it costs me next to nothing as the basic ingredients are really cheap. The enterprise covered its start-up costs years ago."

He was looking so glum that I wondered whether I'd been too hard on him. I laid a comforting hand on his shoulder.

"Do you really think Billy would stop coming in if we didn't offer your special cream? He doesn't come here for alcohol, he's got The Bluebird for that. He doesn't even drink much there unless someone else is buying. He comes out to be with people, to be with friends, instead of on his own at home. I think we should take this letter as a sign to ditch the hooch. In any case, the profits from your new Curiosities Shop will more than make up the deficit from lost cream sales."

When Hector raised his head, I thought he was going to tell me to mind my own business, it was his shop, not mine. But instead, he smiled weakly and put his hand over mine, still on his shoulder.

"Come on, then, Sophie, let's seize the moment before I change my mind. I just hope we're making this nun happy, wherever she is."

I followed him to the stockroom where he kept the still and the supplies inside a locked wooden cupboard.

"I'm still wondering whether she's from one of the convents Auntie May wrote about. Perhaps she told one of the nuns about her involvement with your shop."

Hector unlocked the secret cupboard and took out four full flagons of the ivory liquid.

"You empty these down the tearoom sink, Sophie, while I dismantle the still. I'll take the parts over to the glass recycling bin by the Village Hall."

By the time I returned, he seemed more cheerful. "Of course, I ought to be focussing all my efforts on making the Curiosities Shop work. Although we've got plenty of old books to start it up, eventually I'll need to spend some time out of the shop looking for new stock, and not just at car boot sales, fun as they are. I could hook up with the house clearance company, Joe Snow's, down in Slate Green, for example. When in the past Joe's asked me to take old books off his hands, I've always said no. I'll phone him in the morning to arrange a meeting."

He took me into his arms and held me close, stroking my hair. As I pressed my head against his shoulder, I shed a few surreptitious tears of relief. Until now, I hadn't realised how anxious his hooch had been making me. For the first time it dawned on me that as the person who served it up in the tearoom, I was an accessory to the crime.

"Of course, you know what else this means," Hector was saying. "If we're going to ramp up the Curiosities Shop, we might need another intern to do the donkey work upstairs. Call me selfish, but I'm half hoping Anastasia fails her A Levels so she doesn't go off to university in October. My goodness, Sophie, I don't know what I'd do without your business brain sometimes." He gave me a little squeeze. "You're almost as smart as Tommy!"

When he pulled away and took my face in his hands to see the effect his teasing had had on me, his expression fell.

"Sweetheart, why the tears? I didn't really mean it about Tommy."

I closed my eyes in hope of stemming the flow. What on earth could I say without admitting that I was jealous of Anastasia?

"I'm just so happy you're ditching the hooch," I lied.

He held me close again, kissing my hair.

"I'd have got rid of it sooner, if I'd realised how much it was upsetting you."

I hoped Anastasia had studied very, very hard for her exams.

19 Clean Sweep

I had to smile when Hector suggested that we celebrate Hector's House going on the wagon with a drink at The Bluebird. But first, we decided to take a walk in the early evening air to cool down.

After locking up the shop, we headed out of Wendlebury, across the fields to the spot where the previous autumn, the village had staged a Halloween party, despite the ban imposed by the strange new vicar, Mr Neep. How different the countryside had looked back then, as we waded down the muddy track to Stanley's dark barn, surrounded by skeletal trees. Now all was green and golden, the ripening crops rippling like water in the gentle breeze, a fluttering soundtrack coming from the dense foliage.

Hector and I had looked very different that night, too. Keen to promote the bookshop during the October school holidays, we had dressed as Beauty and the Beast, Hector in full-head lion mask and evening dress, me in a velvet ballgown. We'd hired our costumes from the village shop, costume-making being one of Carol's sidelines to boost her income. I hadn't known Hector well then. It was only our second date, and it was a wash-out, through no fault of our own. At the end of the evening, he'd left me at my front door with nothing more than a paternal kiss. At least he'd taken off his mask for it.

Tonight my Indian dress was almost as long as the ballgown had been.

Hector squeezed my hand. "Do you remember the last time we walked down this way together?"

"I was just thinking about that."

My voice sounded small beneath the big, open sky.

Hector's phone beeped, and he pulled it out of his back pocket and read the message.

"Sorry, Sophie, this will have to be a quick stroll and an even quicker drink. Mum wants me to pop down tonight to get something out of the loft for her. She won't let my dad go up ladders."

"But they live in a bungalow. He wouldn't have far to fall."

"No, but I bounce better than he does. Besides, she's got a spare son, but only one husband."

The memory of meeting Hector's identical twin brother Horace at their parents' house back in January cheered me up. I liked Horace – so similar to Hector in appearance, but so unlike him in other ways, including living on the other side of the world in Australia.

"You're very welcome to come with me, if you like," Hector went on. "You know Mum and Dad are always pleased to see you."

Was that because I reminded them of their old friend May Sayers? I looked down. I certainly would in this dress.

Hector could tell I wasn't keen.

"We could have a stroll along the seafront while we're there, get some fish and chips and a bit of sea air to blow away the cobwebs."

Did I look like I was covered in cobwebs? I pulled irritably at the bodice of my dress.

"No thanks, Hector. I think I'll spend a quiet evening working on my novel in my garden."

He would hardly dissuade me from writing.

"OK, sweetheart, I understand. But before I go, let's have a swift half at The Bluebird."

***

By the time we arrived, The Bluebird had already opened. Several clusters of people were sitting at the picnic tables on the forecourt, enjoying the evening sun. We exchanged friendly greetings with those we knew and, as is the village custom, said hello to those we didn't recognise.

While Hector went inside to fetch our drinks – half-pints of shandy to quench our thirst without making him unfit to drive to Clevedon – I settled down at the next table to a couple of unfamiliar men in their forties, one dark haired, the other salt-and-pepper grey.

"Cheer up, love, it might never happen," said the dark one. "Would a crisp help?"

He offered me the packet, and I took one to be polite.

"I'm OK, thanks, just a bit tired." I didn't want to appear standoffish. "Are you on holiday in Wendlebury? Staying locally?"

When they burst out laughing, I realised what a stupid question this was. They were clearly here on business, in branded grubby navy overalls scarred with splashes of bleach.

"No, love, we've just finished a job," said the grey one. "We thought we'd sit here for a bit and enjoy the sunshine to allow the rush hour to die down before we head back into town."

"I don't blame you," I replied. The thought of commuting into a city instead of walking to work in the village did not appeal to me one bit. Most villagers have to commute, as there aren't many jobs in Wendlebury. I appreciate my good fortune. "Where have you been working? Down on Stanley's farm?"

The grey one, whose eyes crinkled at the corners as he spoke, pointed to the logo on his chest pocket. I squinted against the sunshine.

"Clean Bee," I read aloud. "Oh, you must be the deep cleaning firm my friend at the village school told me about. I don't envy you that task, even if it is only once a year."

I braced myself for sinister revelations, despite their cheery demeanour. Out of the corner of my eye, I saw Hector emerge through the pub's front door, carrying our drinks and a plate of ham sandwiches on a tin tray.

"Believe me, love, we've seen a lot worse," said the dark one. "Besides, at least the grime out here is fresh country dirt."

Hector set the tray on our table and sat on the bench opposite mine for balance.

"Evening," he said affably to the strangers, then looked to me for an introduction.

"These gentlemen have just completed the school's deep clean," I explained. When Hector glanced quickly at me, I realised he was thinking the same thing as I was. If there was a dead body on the premises, surely they would have found it?

"And there's us feeling sorry for ourselves for having to slave away in a hot bookshop, eh, Sophie?"

"Ah, but that's the great thing with this job," said the dark cleaner, draining his glass. "Every day's different. Wherever we're sent, be it a gloomy old church or a grimy factory, we know we're only ever there till close of play. No two days are the same. That's why I love it, don't you, Mike?"

His mate nodded. "Gordon's right. Mind you, today's been the type of assignment we like best – scenic drive to and from work, lunchbreak outdoors with lovely views across fields, and a good old-fashioned pub for a quick one at the end of the day. Plus we only found one dead body at the school, which is a bonus in our line of work."

My shandy went flying across the table, drenching my dress and Hector's bare knees. Fortunately, it missed the plate of sandwiches. Without speaking, Hector stood my glass up and tipped half of his drink into it so I wouldn't go without.

I kept my voice too low to be heard beyond our table. "A dead body?"

Mike and Gordon looked at each other and laughed.

"Yes, but it was only a field mouse, love," said Gordon. "Mike's winding you up. And don't worry, we gave him a decent burial out on the playing field."

"Well, in the compost heap, anyway," added Mike. "A lot easier to dig than the sun-baked ground would be just now. Those guys installing the new playground don't have an easy job in these conditions. What we all need is a good thunderstorm to soften everything up again. I couldn't pull so much as a lettuce in my garden last night, the ground's so hard."

"Couldn't pull a lettuce!" Gordon chortled as he glanced at his watch. "That's a good one! Anyway, we'd better make tracks now, Mike, or we'll miss the start of the cricket highlights on telly."

They were just getting to their feet when Donald swung by with a tray, collecting empties.

"Thanks for dropping by, gentlemen," he said affably, no doubt happy to be doing such good business so early in the evening. He'd had a slow start to the year businesswise, until Ella and I staged a special Valentine's event for him; a country pub is always a precarious business. "See you again, I hope. Maybe come back out for a Sunday lunch with your other halves one weekend? We're famous for our Sunday lunch."

"Don't mind if I do, mate," said Gordon.

"Cheers, m'dears," said Mike, and they sloped off towards the pub car park.

Donald eyed the dark patch all down my front.

"Shall I get a cloth for your dress, Sophie?" he said as he put the men's empties on his tray.

"That's very kind of you, Donald, but don't worry. It'll dry in the sun soon enough, and I'm not stopping long. Thanks anyway."

As soon as Donald moved away, I reached my arms across the table towards Hector. He set down his glass and took my hands in his, giving them a reassuring squeeze.

"If they didn't find a dead man at the school, Sophie, no-one will."

20 Home Alone

When I let myself in at my front door, there was no sign of Blossom, but I soon found her sunning herself on the patio, her black fur mopping up the heat the stone slabs had stored from the scorching sunshine.

Counting the pub's ham sandwiches as my tea, I decided not to bother cooking. Instead, after collecting my notebook, fountain pen and a cold white wine spritzer, I settled down at the patio table to immerse myself in my story. Writing my account of coming to live in the village provided a welcome escape from the day's developments.

I'd just reached the point of describing Hector, dressed in a toga as Homer at last year's Village Show. His skirt had been shorter than the long, loose frock I had been wearing that day for my part as Virginia Woolf on the Wendlebury Writers' float, and the Indian dress I was wearing now.

My thoughts were interrupted by a heady fragrance, reminding me of the floral displays in the produce tent on Village Show day. Surely I wasn't starting to have olfactory hallucinations? An old school friend, now a mental health nurse, once told me they are a bad sign.

"Good evening, my dear." I'd been so intent on my story that I hadn't noticed Joshua entering my garden via the gate in the wall. "I cannot tell you how many times I saw your dear aunt scribbling away in just that position, as deep in her thoughts as you were. I am so glad to see you are following in her footsteps."

I lay down my pen to accept his proffered bunch of roses, their petals a marbled mix of deep peach and raspberry pink. I thought at once of peach melbas.

"Thank you, Joshua, they're beautiful. Can I tempt you to join me in an ice-cream?"

I pulled back my chair and swung my legs out from under the table.

"I'd like that very much, my dear, thank you."

Hanging his walking stick on the side of the table, he lowered himself into the chair beside mine and rested his hands on his thighs. He was still wearing his usual shirt, pullover and tweed jacket.

A few minutes later, we were each enjoying a sundae of vanilla ice-cream topped with chopped fresh peaches from my fruit bowl and a handful of raspberries from the canes at the bottom of the garden. With my first spoonful, I managed to drop an over-ripe raspberry down my front, leaving a juicy pink trail on the bodice before it came to rest in my lap. I popped the errant raspberry back into my bowl, conscious of Joshua watching me out of the corner of his eye. Who was he seeing, me or Auntie May?

I scrubbed at my skirt with a fingertip but only made the pink juice spread.

"Dear me, I hope it doesn't stain," I sighed.

Joshua smiled.

"I'm sure May's dress saw a lot worse on her travels."

That made me want to take it off straight away.

"So is all well at Hector's House?" he continued, his eyes twinkling. Did he mean with the business or with our relationship?

I played it safe.

"Actually, there's exciting news. I've persuaded him to start selling the second-hand books stored in his spare room as a sideline. It will help keep the business in profit."

Joshua nodded in approval.

"The books he has in stock are mostly vintage rather than antique, but many of them have a unique feature that makes them collectible."

"Collecting old books is all very well if you're going to reread them, but if they're lying unopened, gathering dust, you might as well make money from them. Besides –" Joshua's eyes twinkled "– you never know when he might find another use for that room."

My hand flew to my waistline, smoothing the loose folds of my dress to emphasise my flat stomach. "Oh, he's not looking to empty the room. He'll be restocking it from house clearance agents, low-budget auctions, that sort of thing, as his current stock sells. Second-hand sales will be a permanent part of the business."

"Agents? Auctions?" Joshua sat up straighter. "No need for that. He could accumulate a lot of stock simply by asking around the village, starting with me. I have a lot of old books that belonged to my parents, but I shall never read them again. I only keep them because it's too hard to dispose of them. I had thought of taking a bag at a time on the bus to the charity shop at Slate Green, but I fear it may be too strenuous."

The thought of frail old Joshua trying to lug a heavy bag of books on the bus made me anxious.

I scraped my spoon around my bowl to capture the last delicious juices.

"Hector would be happy to take them off your hands, if you're sure."

I hesitated, wondering whether to mention a price. Hector hadn't yet talked me through the business model for his curiosities shop. Would he expect people to donate books or would he buy them?

Joshua solved the immediate problem unprompted.

"I shan't want any money for them. I shall just be glad to gain some shelf space. One less thing for my nephew to sort out once I'm gone."

My spoon clattered into my empty bowl.

"Please don't say that! I'm sure that won't be necessary for a very long time."

Although I wasn't sure at all.

He set his empty bowl on the table beside mine and patted my hand.

"Don't you worry, my dear, such considerations give an old fellow comfort rather than distress. I think of it as packing for my holidays: discarding excess baggage and keeping only what I need for my onward journey. I can't tell you how happy it made dear May when she decided to leave you her cottage, lock, stock, and barrel. Saved her an awful lot of worry, especially towards the end."

I squeezed his hand, unable to find the words to express my gratitude for that little nugget of knowledge. Two years before, unbeknown to me in Germany, and my parents in Inverness, Joshua had nursed May through her final illness, which she'd never revealed to us.

Joshua broke the silence.

"Not that May would want you to feel obliged to live in her cottage forever, or even to stay in Wendlebury. She just wanted to gift you an advantage in life."

At last I found my voice. "It was advantage enough to have her as my aunt."

Gently, he withdrew his hand from mine and reached for his stick.

"Well, well, my dear, I must be getting on. Thank you for the delicious ice, and tell young Hector he is welcome to peruse my parents' library at any time. And don't forget the Longfellow."

After a couple of false starts, he hauled himself up from his chair, raised his Panama hat in farewell, and headed slowly for the gate in the wall. Still thinking of Auntie May, I closed my eyes to keep in the tears, the inside of my eyelids glowing in shades of peach melba as the evening sun warmed my face.

21 Chip Stop

Only when the sun was dropping behind the high holly hedge at the end of my garden did I gather up my things and return indoors. When I set the empty sundae dishes on the kitchen floor, Blossom dashed in to lick the creamy residue. Her black muzzle was ringed pinky-white until she'd sat down and given her face a thorough wash.

Feeling sun-kissed and mellow, I wandered into my little sitting room and flicked on the television, where the local news bulletin was just beginning. As I settled down on the sofa, Blossom leapt onto my lap, her kneading claws pricking my thighs through the flimsy cotton dress.

The newscaster had his serious face on.

"A local headteacher has been reported missing from his temporary accommodation," he was saying. "Born and bred in the Cotswold village of Wendlebury Barrow, Mark Fletcher had just moved back to the area from his previous school in Norfolk, where he had been a deputy head for the last five years, prior to taking up his new appointment as head teacher of Hutmarton Primary. While awaiting completion of his house purchase in Hutmarton, he was staying at Briar House Bed and Breakfast, but the landlady became concerned when she realised his bed had not been slept in, nor had he appeared at breakfast, since the weekend.

"Prior to his disappearance, he was in good spirits and was looking forward to starting his new job in his home county. The chairman of Hutmarton's school governors describes Fletcher as a considerate gentleman for whom it would be out of character to depart without notice. His personal possessions are still in his room, and his car remains parked in the street.

"Anyone with any information as to his whereabouts is asked to contact their nearest police station urgently. The local police are now trying to trace his next of kin, currently travelling abroad."

Startled, I seized the remote control and pressed the off switch. Could Mark Fletcher have been our dead body?

I grabbed my phone from the kitchen table and was about to alert Ella when there was a ring at the doorbell. Laying down my phone, I dashed to the front door. Absurdly, I hoped it might be the missing headteacher, suffering from amnesia, wandering through the village in which he'd grown up in search of clues to his identity. I wondered which cottage he'd lived in as a child. He must have known Auntie May. Everyone knew Auntie May, even though she spent most of the year away from the village on her travels.

But it was only Hector, bearing a steaming white paper bundle under his arm.

"Evening, sweetheart. Fancy some chips?" I stood back to let him come in. "As I turned on to the M5 on my way back from Mum and Dad's, it seemed a long time since our sandwiches at the pub, so I called in at the Peace of Cod in Slate Green and picked up a takeaway."

I led him through to the kitchen, and he sat down at the table and began unwrapping the paper of chips. As I fetched a bottle of malt vinegar from the larder, Blossom charged in from the sitting room, hoping the parcel might include fish. Hector curled his arm protectively around the pile of chips. I was glad she didn't jump up on the table to investigate the delicious aroma, as she might have done if we'd been alone.

While I flicked the kettle on and assembled mugs and teabags, I let Hector burble on about his mum and dad's loft ladder issues, wondering how to broach the subject of the missing headteacher. Only when he fell quiet with his mouth full of chips did I update him on the television news story.

I set our mugs of tea on the table and sat in my usual chair opposite his. "Hector, I know who the dead body is," I said in a voice louder than I intended. "It's Mark Fletcher, the new headteacher at Hutmarton Primary School."

He paused, another chip halfway to his mouth.

"What? How? Why?"

Blossom, pacing about my ankles, miaowed loudly. I threw a chip on the floor to pacify her, which she batted across the room, playing chase.

"I just saw on the television news that he's gone missing."

"Really? And what makes you think he's your dead body? Did he look like the dead body you think you saw?"

"The dead body I saw, Hector, not that I think I saw. I did see it."

"So did he? Look like him, I mean?"

My hands flew to my mouth.

"Oh Hector, I was so startled I switched off before they showed his photo. How could I be so stupid?"

129

"Perhaps subconsciously you didn't want your theory disproved. Just like you don't want to believe my concussed builder theory."

I wrapped my hands round my mug for comfort.

"Hector, this is someone's life we're talking about. I'm not going to try to score cheap points against you when the stakes are so high. But we can look online. There are bound to be photos of him on news websites by now."

Hector wiped his greasy fingers on the chip paper before pulling his phone from his pocket.

"I'll look him up, Sophie. You eat some of these chips before they get cold."

A few clicks and a few chips later, Hector held up his phone to show me a pixellated image of Mark Fletcher, blown up from one of those old-fashioned wide-angle photos which show the entire staff and pupils of a school.

I wrinkled my nose. "Is that the best they can do? It's very fuzzy. You'd think it would be easy enough for a news reporter to find someone's picture on social media."

"Not school staff," said Hector. "Teachers like to keep a low profile on social media for fear of harassment."

I knew all about that. When I was teaching, I'd disguised my name and used a photo of me in fancy dress, so that none of my students would be able to track me down. None of the teachers I knew put their real names on their social media accounts.

Hector searched Fletcher's previous school's website for something clearer.

"Looks as if they've been quick off the mark to replace his mugshot with his successor's." Another few clicks. "Hutmarton's not been as swift to add him to their website. They're still showing an image of the acting head, who's been deputy for ages. Bit rude. But as Fletcher was apparently a Wendlebury boy, maybe someone in the village might be able to source a better picture from local records. There are loads of photos taken at the Village Show each year, for a start."

"Boy? He's older than you."

"Yes, actually, now I come to think of it, his name is familiar. He was in the top year at Wendlebury Primary when I was in the youngest class. I only remember him vaguely; I'm not sure I'd recognise him now. Children's looks change a lot between the age of eleven and adulthood."

I took a sip of tea.

"I'll ask Carol when I call in at the shop on my way to work tomorrow. She's bound to remember him. By the way, you know Hutmarton is one of the schools that Wendlebury might merge with under a single head if their rolls keep falling?"

Hector set down his phone and returned his attention to the chips.

"There you go, Sophie, mystery solved. Ella, in the school office, with the hole punch, to protect Wendlebury staff from losing their jobs and our village from losing its school. Then she stashed him in the lost property cupboard until the night before the bin men were due, when she'd get her new boyfriend to give him a fireman's lift into the wheelie bin."

I considered for a moment. "A rounders bat would be more effective than a hole punch, and there are plenty of those in the school sports shed. But honestly, Hector, we shouldn't laugh. It's a serious matter."

Hector shrugged.

"It's just a slow night for news, if you ask me. Typical media, playing it up for all its worth, headlining him as a headteacher rather than a deputy head when he hasn't even started his new job yet. And a hysterical landlady. I bet he turns up again before long, large as life. I wonder whether he's still any good at magic? I remember being really impressed at the school Christmas concert where he did some card tricks and a vanishing act."

I snatched the biggest chip from beneath his hovering hand. Mark Fletcher wasn't the only one who could make things disappear.

22 Headless

"Look, Sophie, we've made the papers!"

Carol held one up, folded back to reveal a brief article headlined *Village School Loses Head*. Inset was a small black-and-white headshot of a beaming tousle-haired man of about forty. His piercing eyes were the sort to follow you round the room.

"It mentions Wendlebury Barrow as well as Hutmarton," she added, fidgeting from one foot to the other in her excitement as I skim-read the story.

I looked up.

"I had better buy a copy for the bookshop, please, Carol. I'm sure Hector would like to read it."

"Yes, of course. I'm sure most people in the village will want to see it. Today's paper's been flying out the door since the news story on telly last night, and at this rate I'm going to run out of copies before the end of the day." She rang up the cover price on the till. "If only I'd known, I could have ordered extra."

I was still gazing at the photograph. "Do you remember him from when he lived in Wendlebury?" I handed her a two-pound coin.

133

"Oh yes, from when he was quite small. Young Markie was that popular, we were all sorry that his family moved away when he started secondary school. Turned out he couldn't stomach the daily bus ride, poor boy. He was that travel-sick, the only option was for them to up sticks and move to Slate Green, to a house within walking distance of the big school. Real shame, it was, as he was a nice bright boy, always top of his class and such good manners, despite hanging round with Billy. He was another of Billy's little helpers; the Tommy Crowe of his day, but less of a loose candle."

I think she meant cannon.

"He had a good work ethic, bless him. He did a paper round for my mum and dad in his last year at the village school and never missed a morning, not like some I could name."

I folded the paper in half to fit it in my basket.

"I wonder why he moved to Norfolk?"

Carol wrinkled her nose in distaste.

"I never could understand that. Fancy preferring a flat place to our nice hilly Cotswolds. Not my cup of tea at all. He was such a happy little boy when he lived here, I always expected him to turn up again somehow at Wendlebury School."

I swallowed. "What do you mean?"

"I mean as a teacher, or even as a student teacher, as soon as he got the chance. He did his training in Bristol, so he could easily have commuted here from there."

I cast my mind back to my own teacher training.

"Student teachers don't get the chance to choose their placements. They just go wherever they're sent."

"Well, then, once he'd qualified. They're always crying out for male teachers in our village schools, aren't they? Positive disintegration, they call it."

She meant discrimination, of course.

"They've had all women teachers at Wendlebury School for years. Ian's the only man on the staff. Not that he counts, being just the caretaker. Last time they were recruiting for a new head, it was rumoured they'd favour a man, whatever women applied." She pulled a tissue out of her apron pocket and wiped it across her brow. "Funny how they call it a head, when really it's a whole body."

I gulped. "Oh well, I'd better get on. Thanks for the paper. I'll drop it back in on my way home."

"Leave the door open on your way out, would you?"

She was overheating already in another Bri-Nylon dress of her late mother's.

"Why don't you take your apron off, Carol? That would cool you down, too."

"Oh, but my pinny's cotton. Cotton's the best thing in this heat."

"Yes, but if it's on top of nylon, its cooling properties will be lost."

Carol clasped her arms across her generous chest in defence. "Surely you're not suggesting I take my dress off?"

Ted, trudging up the aisle from the stockroom carrying a cardboard case of tinned soup, nodded to me in greeting.

"Sounds like I've arrived in the nick of time, love."

I headed for the door.

***

"Well, does he look familiar?" I asked Hector, reading the article again over his shoulder. I clasped my arms across his chest as he peered at the photograph in the paper.

135

He rubbed his chin in thought.

"The hair looks right, but I'm not entirely sure about the rest of him. It was a long time ago that I last saw him. I was only five when he left the village school, and by the time I went up to the secondary, he was in the top class there, so our paths didn't cross much then, either. But I do remember my mum remarking on what distinctive eyes he had. 'Piercing and intelligent,' she said. And I used to admire his teeth. When my baby ones fell out at the front, I hoped my new ones would grow in neat and tidy lines like his, and not stick out like they did on some of the other kids."

Strange how his recollection from over twenty years ago seemed more vivid than mine from just a few days before. But then there was no-one to dispute his description.

"Thing is, Hector, the body I saw had its eyes and mouth closed, so the pictures in the paper and online don't help. It's all a bit of a blur now. Although this picture does look like the handsome type that Ella goes for."

He got up to flip the door sign to open.

"So we're no further forward, really."

I leaned against the counter for a moment. "Do you know, Hector, I wish the whole business would go away, and we could just get on with enjoying the summer. For example, I'd really like to go on another picnic with you after work, but how could we be so frivolous now that we know someone has gone missing?"

Hector ran a hand affectionately down my spine as he passed me on his way back to his stool.

"But Mark Fletcher is only missing, Sophie. It doesn't mean he's dead, and it doesn't mean his is the body you think you saw, whether dead or merely concussed, in the lost property cupboard. Don't go to meet trouble halfway."

I smiled. "That's what Auntie May always used to say."

He tweaked the end of my ponytail.

"Where do you think I got that piece of wisdom from?"

Hearing the church clock chime nine, I headed for the tearoom to don my apron. As I tied the strings around my waist, the ample calico of my Indian dress fell into loose folds.

"I just thought, Hector. Oughtn't we to consider Mark Fletcher's magical powers?"

Hector chuckled. "I think that's overstating them. He wasn't a superhero. He could just manage a little sleight of hand."

I wasn't so easily deterred. "Do you remember him using his powers apart from on stage? Was he by nature a practical joker? The sort who might pretend to be dead to frighten Ella?"

"That wouldn't be very responsible behaviour from a headteacher. Plus it would be a hell of an introduction to someone who might conceivably end up on his staff, if the schools do merge."

"But if he did, it worked."

Hector turned to remove the cash drawers from the safe.

"Anyway, whoever you saw, I'm still convinced he walked away of his own accord. My money is on either a prankster or someone on the move – a tramp or a traveller, or someone wild camping."

He brought my cash drawer over and inserted it into the tearoom till.

"I suppose we do get a lot of strangers passing through on the Cotswold Way, and quite a few have camping gear with them," I considered. "You'd think if anyone was going to spend the night at the school, they'd pitch their tent on the playing field, not doss down in the lost property cupboard. It would be easy enough to squeeze in through a gap in the hedge and pitch a tent, but a lot harder to break into the school building without setting off the alarm."

I filled the water chamber of the coffee maker and took our favourite mugs off the draining board.

"Maybe they were worried that they'd get evicted if anyone spotted them on the field. Besides, they might have wanted to use the facilities. If they'd been wild camping the length of the Cotswold Way, they'd have been glad of the school's toilets and running water."

"You mean like a traveller? Or the Cotswold Way Wanderer?" The latter was a famous sight along the footpath, walking it barefoot in all weathers, all year round. I really wanted to believe Hector's theory, which was becoming more convincing by the minute. "If it was an intruder, maybe they had special knowledge on how to bypass the alarm."

"You mean they might have been a criminal on the run? Practised safe-cracker and lock-buster?"

He glanced at our painted biscuit tin on the wall. If the school's alarm wasn't intruder-proof, I didn't put much faith in our system.

As the first customers arrived, Hector laid the newspaper on one of the tearoom tables for them to read. Meanwhile I got on with laying out fresh cakes and biscuits, ready for the day ahead.

***

"Well, I declare!"

Billy set down his coffee cup before he'd taken so much as a sip.

"I can't believe it's more than twenty years since that young lad was helping me with the graves at St Bride's."

Billy's various odd jobs around the village include maintaining the churchyard and digging the graves. This latter chore always seems to attract young lads. Billy is almost as good at getting volunteers to dig his graves as Tom Sawyer was at persuading his friends to paint his aunt's picket fence. Of course, Billy never lets the boys dig very far down for safety reasons. The walls of a fresh grave can easily collapse and bury the unwary excavator who hasn't learned the special techniques that Billy told me about when we discovered old Mrs Carter unconscious in an open grave back in the spring.

"I heard young Markie had turned teacher and done well for hisself," he continued, looking at me over the top of his reading glasses. "Brightest lad I've ever had help me. Now here he is, vanished. Lost his memory, I suppose. People do that sometimes when they're stressed. I suppose working over in that Norfolk might send someone doolally. He should never have left his home turf. He'll probably turn up when he's calmed down a bit, just like that Agatha Christie did all those years ago."

I sat at the next free table to fold some paper napkins. "You think so, Billy?"

"Sure. He's got until September to sort himself out. Six weeks' holiday before he starts his new job."

Glad Ella wasn't there to hear Billy's erroneous assumption about school staff's summer holidays, as well as his unenlightened attitude to mental health, I wondered whether he could add to Carol and Hector's descriptions.

"So what was he like when you knew him, Billy? A tearaway, like Tommy? A bit of a joker or a prankster?"

Billy laid down the paper and stared into the distance as he considered.

"No more than any young lad. More sensible than most boys of that age, really, but that's not saying much. Sporty, too, and could whistle like a nightingale. I always suspected he'd go far, though not quite as far as that Norfolk."

I wondered what Billy had against 'that Norfolk'. It couldn't have just been its distance. After all, he'd known Hector and Horace since they'd been born, and Horace now lived on the other side of the world, but I'd never heard Billy speak grudgingly of Australia.

"I can't imagine he's done a bunk with school funds, if that's what you're wondering," Billy continued, turning to the sports pages. "He's sound as a bell, that one. But – " he lowered his voice "– put enough stress on it, and even our Great Bell in St Bride's might crack."

Suddenly, the church clock began to strike midday, and I knocked over a sugar bowl in my surprise.

23 Must Try Harder

I couldn't wait for the lunchtime rush to be over so that I could visit the school to catch up with Ella. As I entered her office, I held up the newspaper, folded open at Mark Fletcher's photo.

"So, what do you think? Is this the man we saw in the cupboard?"

I settled down in her visitor's chair as she peered at the image through narrowed eyes. Then she placed paperclips over his eyes and his teeth, to cover up the bits we hadn't seen, and shook her head.

"That's not much help. But here's an idea: let's make photocopies so we can alter his face to see if it looks any more like our dead body."

After a few minutes with a bottle of Tippex and a pencil, we'd created a striking set of artist's impressions of Mark Fletcher with his eyes and mouth closed. I held the one I thought the best match at arm's length.

"I suppose he might have dyed his hair since the photo was taken. I thought it was lighter."

"Or curled it. I'm sure it was straight."

"Smiling as broadly as he was here could alter his appearance significantly, making his cheeks rise up or his nose broaden."

We looked at each other, both frowning.

"It's hardly conclusive," I sighed.

"Besides, why would Hutmarton's new headteacher be on our premises? Assuming he was alive when he arrived, of course. If he wanted to look round his old school, he'd make an appointment, not just pitch up unannounced."

I straightened out a paper clip and starting cleaning my nails abstractedly.

"Hector's got a new theory now, by the way. If the body wasn't one of the builders concussed or messing about, it might have been a traveller taking advantage of your hospitality overnight, oversleeping and scarpering after we'd disturbed him."

Ella threw down her pencil.

"In that case, he was a very heavy sleeper. Not only did I not disturb him when I went to the cupboard, but he was still spark out when you spotted him. Even if this was his first decent night's sleep for a while, surely no-one could sleep through all your shouting?"

Or your music, I thought, but didn't say.

"He might if he were on drugs or drunk."

"Maybe. You know what our big mistake was, Sophie? Not taking his photo on our phones. Then we'd know for sure whether it was Mark Fletcher or someone else, and the police would have to take us seriously."

"Let's not be so hard on ourselves, Ella. How could we have known that he was going to disappear the minute our backs were turned? Dead men don't usually wander off."

Ella picked up the paper to reread the article. "I do hope it wasn't Mark Fletcher. I hadn't actually met him yet, but from what Mrs Broom had heard on the grapevine, he sounded way better than the clown of a deputy who's been acting head at Hutmarton for the last term. She also found out he was an old boy of Wendlebury, and she made me go up to the attic to dig out his school file. I suppose she wanted to know what her new competition would be like."

Ella swivelled her chair to reach into the filing cabinet behind her and pulled out an ancient manilla file with 'FLETCHER, Mark' in faded ink at the top right-hand corner. She extracted a dark blue booklet the size of a school exercise book, opened it at the last page, and slid it across the desk to me.

"Look, he was a complete brainbox, apparently, top of the class in every subject, and very popular all the way up the school. Head boy, too, and quite handsome, as eleven-year-olds go."

Stapled to the front of the booklet, the passport-sized photo was of a boy in school uniform who was recognisably the younger incarnation of the man in the newspaper. He had the same winning smile and direct gaze, though without the facial definition that only comes with maturity, responsibility and the force of gravity for a few decades.

"So you hadn't met him yet in real life?"

"No. He was due to come to a health and safety committee meeting tomorrow, and I was hoping to get into his good books in Mrs Broom's absence. If our schools do merge, there'll only be room for one school business manager, and I intend that one to be me. You know I said the other day I'd been planning to move on to a larger school in a year or two? Staying put when the two small schools combine would be easier.

"However, before you arrived just now, I had an email from that awful deputy I mentioned, saying that under the circumstances, he'll come to the meeting instead. Ugh! David Harman is unbearable – patronising and misogynistic. Just because he's the only male member of staff at Hutmarton, he thinks he's God. And he's also an old boy of our school, so he thinks he knows more about Wendlebury Primary than I do. I was hoping Mark Fletcher would take him down a peg or two."

"Really? I wonder what his school report was like!"

Ella smirked. "Second best to Fletcher, apparently. I brought his file down, too, while I was up in the attic. Don't tell Mrs Broom – I don't want to look unprofessional."

"Ooh, can I see?"

She reached into the filing cabinet again and passed David Harman's report to me. I flicked through it, reading the teacher's comments as we carried on chatting. I was so glad I didn't have to write reports anymore.

"So everything will carry on as normal at Hutmarton until Fletcher turns up?" I asked.

"Sure. The six weeks of the summer holidays will soon fly by, and they'll still have to get everything done. They can't have the kids coming back to half-finished maintenance and curriculum jobs in September, any more than we can. Anyway, enough about school. I need distracting. How's your intern getting on?"

I pulled a face.

"Hector's smitten with her. He's hoping she'll fail her A Levels so she can stay on at the shop instead of going to uni."

Ella gasped. "Poor girl. He can't be serious."

I shrugged. "Well, what am I to think? She's meant to be in his flat on her own all day cataloguing his old books. Next thing I know, he's up there sharing an iced coffee she's rustled up for him while leaving her lip gloss all over his tumblers. It feels almost as if she's moved in with him."

Ella clasped her hands in glee.

"Ooh, do you think she's got a crush on him? Do you think when she's alone up there she raids his wardrobe and sniffs his clothes? Gets into his bed and rolls around between his sheets?"

I clapped my hands to my mouth in horror.

"Ella! Please! I hadn't even thought of that."

Ella waved dismissively.

"Oh, lighten up, Sophie. I'm only teasing. She's just a kid."

"Yes, but a very clever, very pretty kid. And very pleasant, too, damn her. Like our missing friend, Mark Fletcher, she has plenty of winning traits."

Ella looked me up and down.

"Well, you could help your own cause by not wearing your dead aunt's chintzy frocks for a change."

I followed her gaze.

"It's not chintz, it's cheesecloth: timeless Indian hippy chic. And sooo comfy in this heat."

Ella raised her eyebrows. "Voluminous hippy chic. It's got as much fabric as a hot air balloon. Anyway, my point is, if you want to fend off your teenage rival, stop channelling your inner old lady. Remember you're the same generation as Hector, not his gran."

"What do you want me to do, come to work in a vest top and mini skirt like Anastasia?"

Ella snorted with laughter. "Now there's a plan. Poor Anastasia! Do you think she was named after the mysterious daughter of the last Tsar of Russia? That doesn't bode well."

I shuffled my chair back and stood up.

"Nor does my spending too long away from the shop. I'd better get back, Ella. Good luck with your meeting tomorrow. Let me know if you hear any news of the missing head. At least if he does turn up, we can rule him out as our invisible friend."

As I turned onto the High Street, I stepped back from the slipstream of a bright yellow lorry – a concrete transporter, its mixer slowly spinning as it headed for Hutmarton. Finding this vehicle suspicious, I scrabbled in my pocket for my phone to take a photo of its licence plate, but by the time I had opened the camera, the lorry was out of sight.

***

"Just because a crime is really obvious doesn't mean someone wouldn't do it," I protested. "Burying a body beneath the patio may have become a cliché since it featured on that soap opera years ago, but it's still the perfect place to hide one."

Hector did not reply as he flipped the door sign to closed.

"Don't you think it's worth checking out where that concrete lorry was going?" I persisted. "I've never seen one in the village before, and it seems an extraordinary coincidence that it should arrive just as a dead body disappears." I sighed. "I should have memorised its licence plate instead of wasting time trying to photograph it. Have you heard of anyone laying a new patio in the village? Or of any other concreting job in Wendlebury?"

146

Hector stroked his chin in mock thought.

"You mean like motorway flyovers? Dams? Not this week."

I gave his arm the slightest of slaps. "Now you're just being silly. Let's go for a walk around the village this evening to see if we can spot anything suspicious."

Hector shook his head.

"What's the point? You won't be able to tell from the road whether anyone has been laying a patio in their back garden."

"Concrete lorry tyre prints on their drive? Besides, it doesn't have to be a patio. They could be resurfacing their front drive or building an extension or a sandpit or a pond or getting their cellar tanked against the damp. Or building one of those structures where they pour concrete between shuttering to create foundations."

Hector laughed as he began to cash up.

"Have you been binge-watching home improvement shows?"

I frowned. "Have you got this month's parish magazine to hand? I can check the list of planning applications. That should narrow it down a bit."

"No, sorry."

Hector carried on stacking pound coins.

"So, are you coming to mine tonight?" he said once he'd dropped them into coin bags and stowed them in the safe.

"No, I think I could do with an early night on my own, thank you."

An early night alone with time to think, nestled between cool linen sheets laundered thin and supple by Auntie May, seemed very appealing indeed.

24 Tanked

Next morning just before elevenses, Hector slammed the phone down and shouted across the shop floor to me.

"Sophie, emergency at the school! Quick, action stations!"

Laying out the fresh cakes beneath their glass domes, I turned to stare in alarm before clocking his impish grin.

"Ella needs cake, and she needs it fast!" he continued in the same tone.

My shoulders dropped and I breathed again, although my heart was still pounding.

"You idiot, Hector, you really frightened me for a moment. Why so urgent?"

He leaned back on his stool. He'd been hunched over his keyboard for the last half hour, typing furiously on his latest novel.

"Apparently Ella had a flat tyre on the way to work this morning, and by the time she'd fixed it, she was too late to call in at the village shop to pick up cakes. She's got Kate and a few other visitors coming in for a health and safety meeting, and she wants to butter them up. I don't know why she didn't just ask Kate to fetch them."

I took a flat-pack cardboard cake box out of the cupboard and started to fold it into shape.

"Ella wouldn't want Kate to think her inefficient. She's going to ask Kate to be her referee next time she applies for a job. Which might be soon if the council decides to merge Wendlebury School with Hutmarton."

"Surely they'd merge at Wendlebury rather than Hutmarton? Our school's bigger, and it also had a much better report than Hutmarton's at their most recent inspection. Then they'd be more likely to keep her on."

I shrugged. "On the other hand, Wendlebury's is by far the older building. If they take maintenance and fuel costs into account, Hutmarton might be the more viable long-term option."

"I suppose so. I don't think the fabric of Wendlebury School's changed much since Horace and I were pupils, and it wasn't in great nick then. Still, it would be awful if it closed. It is our biggest single customer in the local education sector. Hutmarton has never ordered one book from us."

"Apart from that, Wendlebury School must have played a big part in the lives of so many villagers for generations."

Saddened by the thought of its possible closure, I filled the box with a generous helping of our most luscious cakes.

"I won't be long, I'll just drop these off and come straight back," I said as I passed the trade counter on my way out. "No need to call Anastasia down to run the tearoom."

As I headed towards the school, I regretted putting that idea into his head.

***

149

The scent of the strawberry tarts wafted up through the cardboard, making me glad I'd left a couple in the fridge for me and Hector later on. As I reached the school gate, I took a deep breath to savour the sweet almost floral fragrance, and instantly regretted it as a big bright-green tanker rumbled to a halt beside me.

'Suction Master – septic tanks and cesspits cleansed with a smile,' said the slogan on the side in a playful red and yellow typeface. I'd already guessed its business from the smell.

A burly suntanned man with a shaven head leaned out of the nearside window.

"Morning, love. You with the school? Can you tell me where you want us?"

A heckle from the driver was too muffled for me to understand, which was probably just as well.

"If you've come to empty the septic tank, the access is in the playground at the top of the playing field." Thinking it might not help Ella's charm offensive to greet visitors with the aroma of sewage, I took charge. "You're probably best driving down the track at the side and going in through the five-barred gate, rather than parking here. The contractors working on the playground will point you in the right direction."

The man gave me a friendly wave of thanks.

"Good call, love. We've got a long enough hose to reach the septic tank from here, but we prefer not to take it across the public thoroughfare if there's another way. Health and safety, and all that."

"I'm just going into the school office, so I can tell the business manager you're here," I offered. "Any particular message?"

"Just ask him to come out to sign off our paperwork when the noise stops, love. Save us tramping through the building."

"Her," I corrected him. "The business manager is a woman."

But the lorry had already begun to move off.

***

Ella's office was empty, but I bumped into Ian in the entrance hall.

"I've just sent the Suction Master lorry round the side entrance," I told him. "I hope I did the right thing."

He rubbed his hands together.

"Oh good, they were meant to be here Friday afternoon, just after the kids had gone home for the holidays. I was getting worried they'd hold up work on the playground. As it is, the contractors have had to delay their tarmac delivery for the base layer until tomorrow."

Just then, the front doorbell rang, and I opened it to Kate, who was dressed in a dark business suit. A glossy leather folio the colour of freshly fallen conkers was tucked under her arm.

"Are you here for the meeting, too, Sophie, in your capacity as school librarian?"

I had no idea I'd been officially designated as such, but if that's what Ella had told Kate, it was fine by me. There's a tendency in this village for voluntary roles to be thrust upon you without you realising until you are committed. That was how the vicar signed me up to teach his Sunday School classes.

"Actually, I've just come to bring cakes from Hector's House to fuel your discussions."

151

I lifted the lid of the box, and Kate peered in, licking her lips.

"Yum! What a kind donation. You know how to look after your customers. Thank you, Sophie."

I had been planning to leave the till receipt on Ella's desk for her to settle later, but now I scrunched it up to throw in the nearest bin. I followed Kate to the school hall, where I could hear someone arranging a table and chairs for the meeting.

The French doors had been flung wide to admit the fresh morning air from the playing field, and a pleasant breeze was rippling the stage curtains. At the far end of the hall, the serving hatch from the school kitchen was open, and the hot water urn was bubbling cheerfully. Ella was in the kitchen, flinging open cupboard doors. At the sound of our footsteps across the parquet floor, Kate's court shoes clicking, my sandals squeaking, she turned to greet us.

"Hello, you two, you're a welcome sight. Kate, take a seat. You'll find the meeting papers on the table. Sophie, could you please stay a moment to give me a hand?"

She looked so anxious that I cast aside my worries about Anastasia usurping my position and went to join her in the kitchen. At least the sight of my box of cakes cheered Ella up a little.

"Oh, Sophie, I'm all behind after that wretched business with my tyre this morning. Could you please just find half a dozen cups, saucers and cake plates? Oh, and serviettes, milk jug and sugar bowl, and make us some flasks of coffee? After all, catering is your field of expertise, not mine. You'll make a better job of it than I would."

Now she was pushing her luck. But Ella is my friend, she was having a hard day, and this meeting was important to her, so I let her off.

A tall man of about forty with close-cropped hair had just arrived and was shaking hands with Kate.

"Go on, go and look after your visitors," I told Ella. "But you'd better shut the doors to the playground as you go past and open the windows on the other side of the hall instead. Your septic tank's about to be emptied. The tanker arrived at the same time as I did. The man said when the noise stops, can you please go out and sign off his paperwork."

Ella grimaced. "Talk about bad timing!" She glanced at her watch. "I don't suppose you could do that for me, too, please? Not empty the tank." I was glad there were some limits. "Close the doors and open the windows, I mean. That guy who's just arrived is David Harman, Hutmarton's condescending deputy head, and I don't want him taking me for support staff."

With that, she darted across the hall to greet him before I could protest.

***

I set two plates of cakes equidistant from the six people now seated around the table. As well as Ella, Kate, and David Harman, the other three were Mr Barnard, a Hutmarton school governor, and two local councillors, a Mrs Digweed and a Mr Grant. I tried not to look out of the window, hoping the visitors might not notice the Suction Master hose snaking its way across the playground towards the manhole cover amid raucous cries from the playground workmen.

153

"So how are each of your schools implementing the new annual deep clean policy?" Councillor Digweed was asking as I laid a plate and cake fork beside her papers.

Ella had her answer ready.

"All done. Completed on Tuesday, using the best of the three companies invited for competitive tender in May."

David Harman scowled.

"Ours is due for late August. Far better to do it later in the summer break. That leaves less time for the premises to get dirty before the children arrive. Plus, of course, I want our new headteacher to be involved." He put up his hands. "Although who knows when that might be now following Tuesday night's news. I trust you've all heard of his mysterious disappearance?"

The others nodded.

"Now, now, David," said Mr Barnard. I hoped the rest of the Hutmarton governors were more effectual.

"It's probably just a misunderstanding about his starting date," said Kate, ever the diplomat. "After all, it is the silly season in the press. The landlady at his lodgings might just have invented his disappearance to promote her business during the peak holiday season. Stranger things have happened."

If that was the case, I questioned the landlady's wisdom. Who would want to stay at a bed and breakfast from which a previous guest had mysteriously vanished? It would be like booking a haircut at Sweeney Todd's.

Councillor Digweed raised her pen for attention. "Yes, to be honest, at the council we're rather cross that the press have seized on it as a story. It's hardly helpful to our department, or to the school community, or indeed to the poor man himself to have his face all over the papers. He's quite at liberty to spend a night away from his lodgings if he wishes. It's not as if the fellow had been electronically tagged by the police and put under curfew. He is probably just catching up with old friends in the area after living away for so long, and good luck to him."

"That's the local rag for you, always desperate for a story," put in her colleague, Councillor Grant. "Pure commercialism at its worst. They've seen that he's an old boy of Wendlebury and new headteacher of Hutmarton and realised they'll get bumper sales in both villages for as long as the story runs."

"I'm an old boy of Wendlebury, too, don't forget," David Harman interjected, at which they all looked surprised. He shrugged. "I know, no-one ever remembers me like they do Fletcher, because I was never head boy or games captain. But I was still a credit to the school."

When Kate reached across the table to pat his hand, he jumped at her touch.

"And you still are. How wonderful it will be to have two top scholars from Wendlebury leading the fray at Hutmarton."

"That should make any merger a little easier, if and when it happens," murmured Councillor Grant to Councillor Digweed, who put a finger to her lips to caution him against indiscretion.

"Anyway, I am more than happy to hold the fort until Fletcher deigns to put in an appearance," David Harman continued. "That's what deputy heads are for, isn't it? I'll be Lyndon B Johnson to Fletcher's JFK. Do you know which of those two held the office of president for longer?"

Ella narrowed her eyes at him. "Only because JFK got shot. In history's eyes, Johnson will always be JFK's deputy."

David Harman did not smile back. "My point is that Wendlebury is disadvantaged by not having a deputy head."

Ella laid her pen on the table and straightened her back.

"As you well know, David, our governors decided to deploy their budget differently here. They traded management hours for more contact time with pupils. I'm perfectly capable of managing the previous deputy head's admin, leaving the teachers to concentrate on teaching. Which is why our pupils do so well. Now, I'm sure the councillors and governors are keen to make the best use of their time with us, so perhaps we might tackle the agenda, please."

"Hear, hear," said Mr Barnard.

I brought two large flasks of coffee from the kitchen and set one on the table, filling everyone's cups from the other. Just as I'd finished, there was a tap at the French doors. I turned to see Ian, unusually agitated, waving at me urgently.

Ella shot me an anxious look.

"I'll see what Ian wants, Ella," I said, trying to sound calm. "You carry on with your meeting."

As soon as I'd opened the French doors and closed them behind me, Ian leaned down to whisper in my ear. Behind him, I could see the two Suction Master men in their emerald-green overalls, alongside the trio of playground workmen, all grim-faced, clustered around the manhole that gave access to the septic tank. It was strange to see the naturally garrulous group of workmen silenced. The end of the hose lay abandoned a few paces behind them on the ground, its dripping nozzle slowly creating a small brown puddle on the hopscotch grid.

"Ian, will you tell them indoors or shall I? I will if you want me to."

Ian gave a sigh of relief. "Oh, Sophie, would you? In the meantime, I need to fetch some more rubber gloves." He turned to call over his shoulder. "Hang on, lads, I'll be right back."

25 Discharged

Returning to the hall, I walked to the meeting table as slowly as I could without seeming eccentric, my heart pounding so hard I was surprised no-one else could hear it. Kate, who had watched me come through the French doors, gave me an encouraging smile.

"Everything OK out there, Sophie?"

David Harman, sitting with his back to the window, turned round to look at me, no doubt ready with some put-down, but instead of speaking, he stared out into the playground at the men in green.

"I thought you were getting your septic tank emptied last week, Ella? That's what you said at our last meeting." I didn't see that it was any business of his. "Still, if you will use Suction Master instead of the firm I recommended, I'm not surprised you're having problems. Bunch of amateurs. I recommend you call them off right now. They're clearly making a complete hash of the job."

I didn't envy Ella having to sit through a whole meeting with such a rude, combative man. Except now the meeting would likely be cut short.

"Our contractors at Hutmarton are very good," said Mr Barnard, proving at last that he could say more than two words at a time.

Councillor Grant coughed. "So long as there were three competitive tenders, Ella –"

"We've been using Suction Master as long as I've been here," asserted Ella. "We've never had any cause for complaint before."

"Actually, it's not Suction Master that's the problem," I said slowly. I was in no hurry to make my announcement, especially in front of Ella's guests. But with everyone staring at me now, I could put it off no longer.

I chose my words with utmost care.

"I'm afraid it's not Suction Master's fault that they're unable to start the outflow from the tank –"

"Of course, Hutmarton's been on mains drainage for years," David Harman interrupted. "Makes a huge difference to our overheads, and it's more hygienic, too. We don't have to fool around with this nonsense."

Verbal diarrhoea, I diagnosed, before realising what an unfortunate analogy it was in the circumstances.

"Mr Harman, kindly let the young lady finish, please," said Councillor Digweed, not taking her eyes off me. "So what is the problem, exactly? It's common knowledge that blockages occur if a septic tank is left unemptied too long."

In her indignation, Ella's voice rose half an octave.

"I've had it emptied every summer, without fail, as long as I've been here. It can't have compacted."

At least I could put her mind at rest on that score.

"No, it's something else blocking the hose. Something rather more awful than that. I'm sorry to tell you that when the Suction Master men shone a torch down there just now, they found a dead body, floating on the very top of the waste matter."

Ella's jaw dropped. "Not another one!" she exclaimed, before clapping her hands over her mouth to silence herself.

"Another one?" cried Councillor Digweed. "Whatever do you mean, Ella?"

For a moment, Ella froze.

"I'm so sorry, I was just making a joke in very bad taste."

"Lordy!" said David Harman. "Perhaps we should reconvene another time rather than continue with all this disruption."

Ella covered her face with her hands.

"I'm so sorry." She splayed her fingers just enough to look at me through the gaps. I gave a tiny shake of my head to indicate that I would not be giving anything away about 'our' dead body just yet.

David Harman, who had quickly composed his face to look mournful, held up his hands in mock surrender.

"OK, OK. As acting head of Hutmarton School, I realise how devastating it will be for you to find a dead body on the premises. What a fright for the poor kids. Still, if any of them want to transfer to Hutmarton, there's plenty of time between now and the start of the new academic year. We have places available in every year."

"So we do," said Mr Barnard.

Councillor Grant thumped the table hard enough to rattle the crockery.

"Mr Harman, that is a most inappropriate comment. Can we all please remain professional here? Someone has died, and no matter who it is, it is a human life lost, and the victim is some poor mother's son."

"Or daughter," added Kate, her voice cracking with emotion. "Sophie hasn't told us anything about the person's identity yet. Please God, let it not be one of the children."

One by one, they rose to their feet and moved across to the French windows, where Ian was now lowering the library window pole down the manhole and into the murky depths of the septic tank. All were silent, except David Harman, his arms folded like a sulky child whose teacher has just scolded him in front of all the class.

"Well, it's not very professional the way Wendlebury has been poaching our kids all term. Seventeen we've lost since Easter, plus six of our village children are joining their reception class in September."

Ella flushed with rage. "That's hardly our fault. It's commonplace for parents to be nervous whenever there's a change of head teacher. They like to see how the new person settles down, how things shape up under their leadership and what changes they might make before they commit to a school. They know Mrs Broom's not going anywhere, and they value that stability, especially for the all-important first and last years of primary school. Plus we give them a very good experience when they come here to visit on our open days."

David Harman was undeterred.

"Which is exactly why I should have been promoted from deputy to head, so that there would be no change. It's a no-brainer."

"Now, now," said Mr Barnard. "We've had this conversation already. End of story."

David Harman ignored him. "Anyway, where's Mrs Broom when she's needed? Swanning off on holiday leaving the school under the management of someone with no teaching qualifications at all. I don't suppose you've even been to university."

Ella drew herself up to her full height.

"Actually, I've an MSc in nuclear physics."

That silenced him. I tried to look less startled than I felt.

"David, please!" said Mr Barnard, the Hutmarton governor finally showing some spirit. "Your petty career concerns are irrelevant to the matter in hand."

"And Ella! It was Ella too!"

As David Harman pointed accusingly, Ella shifted closer to Kate for moral support.

Kate smiled serenely. "Funnily enough, David, I think I can picture you as a pupil here now, eleven years old all over again. I believe you were in the top class when my godsons, Hector and Horace Munro, were in their first year here."

David Harman disregarded her. He was like a clockwork toy who could not stop until his spring had wound down.

"Anyway, you may have to promote me if Mark Fletcher is dead. You won't get anyone else at such short notice before September. Besides, parents may protest if I'm not made up to head after I've applied three times in the last five years. At least I'm always there. I'm dependable. They know I won't let them down."

Councillor Digweed gasped. "What an extraordinary assumption. Whatever made you leap to the conclusoconclude that Mr Fletcher is dead?"

David Harman strolled back to the table to collect his coffee cup and took a long drink before he replied.

"I'm only saying what everyone else is thinking, surely? That the tea lady's dead body out there –"

"He's not my dead body!" I cried.

162

"– that the body in the septic tank is Mark Fletcher's. After all, he is the only local person who has been reported missing. Isn't that what you all thought when the tea lady made her grand announcement?"

"I'm not the tea lady!"

He turned to me, his head on one side. "Don't worry, love, you'll get your fifteen minutes of fame tonight. I bet the local press and TV and radio will all be beating a path to your doorstep. Better go and get your hair done." He looked me up and down. "And put on a smarter outfit."

Kate shut him up at last.

"Actually, no, it is by no means a certainty that the body in the tank is Mark Fletcher. There are two more possibilities."

26 Septic

"The first is a traveller who was last seen at the illegal camp just outside Slate Green," Kate continued. "He was reported missing by his family at the end of last week. They must have been seriously concerned to alert the police, because, as you know, Councillors, Mr Barnard, that particular community wouldn't want to attract the attention of the law unless they were desperate. The missing man is a community elder, fit and wiry for his age, and it is considered out of character for him to disappear without notice.

"The second is a walker of the Cotswold Way. Probably the most famous regular walker of all time, the Cotswold Way Wanderer. He pounds up and down the footpath in all weathers, sleeping rough all year round. Harmless enough, and hardy."

The councillors exchanged glances.

"Yes, we've heard of both of these disappearances," said Councillor Digweed. "I've seen the photofit picture the police put together of the traveller, and I think I'd recognise him easily enough."

"And I've seen the Wanderer a number of times while walking my dog," said Councillor Grant. "So if we're asked to identify the body in the first instance, we can probably oblige. Of course, the next of kin will have to make the formal identification, but between us, we can at least determine whether it is one of those two. That is, if you have the stomach for it, Councillor Digweed?"

Councillor Digweed cleared her throat.

"Yes. Yes, it would be my duty."

I admired their courage.

Still the Suction Master duo in their emerald overalls crouched over the open manhole, looking for all the world like paramedics. Ian and the workmen clustered behind them.

Then a new, shorter figure emerged out of nowhere, darting across from the edge of the field to join them. Squeezing between the Suction Master men, he peered down the hole to see what they were looking at, and for a moment was as still as a corpse himself. Then, skirting round the others, he charged across the playground towards us and crashed through the French doors into the hall.

Tommy, in camouflage shorts and olive-green T-shirt, stood panting on the threshold, leaving the doors wide open behind him, taken aback to see strangers in the hall. I dashed over to check he was OK. He's a robust lad, but seeing his first dead human body must have come as a shock.

Gently I led him outside, but in the opposite direction from the manhole. Ella closed the French doors behind us, both to spare the committee the heady aroma of the open septic tank and to provide privacy and a filter for whatever Tommy had to say.

"I was in my hide," he began, pointing to a dense thicket in the shrubbery at the edge of the playing field. "That's where I made my hide, you see, like Hector said,

165

where no-one would think of looking for me. I've been there loads this week, and I've seen a lot more than birds."

***

As I returned to the school hall, Tommy followed to claim a cream cake as his reward for agreeing to remain silent about what he'd seen until I spoke to him. The committee was still engaged in debate about the likely identity of the mysterious body.

"Of course, the Wanderer's most distinctive feature, apart from his blonde dreadlocks, is his refusal ever to wear shoes," Mrs Digweed was saying.

Ella raised her hand. "Do you mean formal shoes, as opposed to trainers, or any footwear at all?"

"He was always completely barefoot. The soles of his feet were like shoe leather. They'd have to be to cope with his lifestyle. How he never gets frostbite in the snow is beyond me. Same way as my dog, I suppose. It's just normal to him."

"You'd have no trouble identifying the traveller, either, unless he's been in that tank for a very long time," said Mr Barnard. "That's because of all the tattoos on his face. There's hardly a patch of bare flesh to be seen among the roses and ivy and spiders' webs and whatnot. There can't be many men who'd match that description."

Kate clasped her hands decisively.

"Actually, I think we had better wait until the police get here and leave the matter entirely to them."

David Harman got to his feet and turned as if about to head for the entrance hall. I raised my hands to stop him.

"Actually, ladies and gentlemen, I don't think that will be necessary, as it's neither the Wanderer nor the traveller. You see, from what Tommy told me just now, it's unmistakeably the body of a woman."

27 The Bog Person

"It can't be!" cried David Harman, returning to his chair and falling back into it with a thud. His face was suddenly as pale as the pastry of the neglected apple turnover on his plate.

Kate turned to him sharply.

"Why ever not? What do you know that we don't?"

"Nothing. Nothing at all." He slipped his pen into his jacket pocket and scooped his copies of the meeting papers into his folder. "Anyway, it's clear we're not going to get any proper work done with all this disruption. I propose we reconvene at a quieter time – at my school, perhaps?" He forced a smile at the councillors and governors. "I'm sure I can provide you with a calmer setting than this madhouse."

Kate put the cap back on her fountain pen and laid it neatly beside her notebook.

"Actually, I must ask that nobody leaves until the police have arrived. They will doubtless want to question us all. Ella, please go to the office and call them."

David Harman, who had been getting to his feet, sat back down heavily in his seat.

"But why? How could any of us be implicated when we've been sat indoors here the whole time?"

He threw his folder down on the table, knocking over the milk jug, which fortunately was empty.

Kate took no notice of his petulance.

"We've entered territory far beyond the remit of the health and safety committee. Sophie, would you mind awfully making some mugs of tea? I think our friends in the playground could probably do with it."

"Just make sure they wash their hands thoroughly before they drink it," added Councillor Digweed, in the first observation that had any real connection with the health and safety agenda.

***

By the time I took the tea out to the playground, the workmen were tidying their tools away. It would hardly be respectful to carry on with their work in the circumstances.

"Do you think it's OK to have a smoke with my cuppa, love?" asked Dai. "Steady me nerves, like."

I turned to Suction Master's men in green.

"Is it safe to smoke near an open septic tank?" I asked. "Will it be emitting any flammable gases with the top off like that? An explosion is the last thing we need just now."

"Don't worry, mate, we'll go down the bottom of the field, as far away as we can get," put in Dai before they could answer. "It's just that I could murder for a ciggie. Oh, sorry, love, I didn't mean that. I just mean I'm gasping."

For all his usual bluster, Dai's hands were shaking.

"OK, as long as you don't leave the premises. The police will want to question all of us who have been on site today. Just leave everything as it is and enjoy your tea."

"That suits me fine, love," said Dai, cigarette and lighter already in his hands. Robbie and Matt followed him onto the field. I suspected it wasn't the first time they'd sloped off for a smoke during working hours.

"No problem for us either, darling," said one of the Suction Master men, sitting down on the grass. "This was our last job of the day anyway."

"Would you two mind staying here and standing guard over the septic tank until the police arrive? I shouldn't think they'll be long. Just give me a shout if you want any more tea."

"Thanks, darling, will do," said the driver, raising his mug to me in appreciation. His mate stretched out on the grass and closed his eyes, looking disconcertingly like a corpse himself.

As I returned to the hall, Ian was beckoning to me from down the corridor, out of sight of the meeting. I hadn't realised he'd dodged back inside while I was taking the workmen their tea. I hurried to see what he wanted.

"Sophie, can you play for time? I want to check the security cameras from the last week for any sign of intruders dumping the body in the tank. Probably in the last day or two. It looks quite, er, fresh, all things considered."

"Don't you check the cameras on a daily basis anyway?"

He shook his head. "No, they're only there for exception reporting and to keep our insurers happy. If nothing untoward happens, we never look at them. We're all far too busy. It's not like we're a big supermarket or museum with a dedicated team of security staff."

"But won't it take ages to go through all the footage?"

"No. You see, there's a powerful fast-forward function that skips to actual movement, rather than showing you nothing happening in real time."

The school's technology certainly put the bookshop's painted biscuit tin to shame.

"Is there a camera that will have recorded the meeting in the hall, too?"

"Yes, but surely you don't need me to check that, do you?"

"No, but I'd like to be able to show the tape to the police later, as I think it contains crucial evidence from the meeting. So don't wipe it, whatever you do."

"OK, Sophie, though I can't think how it will help. What is it you've got up your sleeve?"

"No time to explain now, Ian. All will become clear later. You go and check that footage, and I'll alert Ella what you're up to before I go back to the hall."

Ella hadn't yet returned after calling the police, so her office was my next stop. As soon as I set foot inside, she darted across for a reassuring hug, her face wet with tears.

"Oh, Sophie! How can there be a second dead body in the same week? And a woman, too! You don't suppose it's Mrs Broom, do you? I feel terrible now. I've been resenting the fact that she's not sent me so much as a text, and all the while she might have been bobbing about in the septic tank. She was going away alone, you see, on a singles holiday, so no-one would have noticed she was missing. The holiday company would just think she'd changed her mind or missed her flight."

With my arms still around her, I said very quietly, "Listen, Ella, don't react, but let me reassure you: there is no second body."

Ella leapt back, wide-eyed.

"Don't tell me the second one's done a bunk, too? Not with all those people standing around? Is there some kind of illusionist playing tricks on us, like those street magicians you see on telly? Are we being secretly filmed by some bad-taste reality show?"

I took her hands in mine and squeezed them in reassurance. Her fingers were as cold as ice cream.

"No, it's nothing like that. But listen carefully. It's not a different body. There is no second body. This is the same one we saw in the cupboard, but messier."

She pulled her hands free of mine and clapped them to her face in surprise.

"But you said this one is a woman? I know our memories of the first body are inconsistent, but neither of us doubted it was a man."

"I know. I lied about it being a woman. I wanted to test Mr Harman's reactions. Didn't you notice what he said when I announced it was a woman? 'It can't be'. I reckon he knows it's a man, and he knows who it is, because he put him there. No wonder he's been so jumpy since he arrived and wants the meeting to be disbanded. He's guilty as sin.

"But don't tell the others just yet. At the moment, you, Ian, Tommy and I are the only ones in the hall who know that the body is a man's, and I've told the workmen to stay outside until the police get here, so they won't let on either."

Ella glanced towards the door.

"Hadn't we better get back quick in case they go outside and find out for themselves?"

"I don't suppose any of them will rush out to inspect a dead body in a septic tank in a heatwave. Even so, we'll have to act fast. Come with me and follow my lead. How much time have we got, by the way, until the police get here?"

"They estimated half an hour. All the local crews are attending a car crash this side of Slate Green, so they had to give that priority as it involves live people. Thankfully there were no fatalities, but it's playing havoc with the traffic."

"Great. Now, let's get back to the hall. Things are about to get interesting."

***

When we returned to the hall, Tommy was making short work of the remaining cakes while tapping away at his phone. I leaned over his shoulder to check what he was doing. I should have forewarned him about confidentiality.

"Tommy, I hope you're not sharing images or information about our discovery online. Please save anything you've got to say about it until the police get here."

"No fear of that, miss, I can't get a signal. Wow, do you think they'll want to question me as a murder witness? Do you think they'll do nice cop, nasty cop, like on telly? I bet they won't make me squeal! Brilliant!"

I suppressed a smile, for once thankful that the village is in a black spot for mobile phone signals. I didn't think for a moment that Tommy might be the murderer, but it didn't stop his vivid imagination going into overdrive.

Everyone else was sitting in silence, avoiding each other's eyes. Councillor Grant was leaning back with his eyes closed but didn't seem to be asleep. I took the spare seat opposite David Harman, beside Ella and Kate. The three of us on the home team had a prime view of the playground. Clasping my hands on the table in front of me, I forced a smile.

"Now, Mr Harman, while you're here, I might as well take the opportunity to chase you up about an inter-school library loan that's still outstanding from last term. It'll save me the bother of emailing you."

He rolled his eyes.

"Overdue library books are hardly a priority right now."

"Ah, but they are." I was starting to enjoy what I later described to Hector as 'the tea lady's revenge'. "You see, I happened to notice at the end of term that you hadn't returned a substantial stack of books you borrowed from Wendlebury School's library at Easter. You said you needed them for a summer-term project, and you left a big gap in our ancient history section."

He gazed around the table, as if looking for an ally, but didn't find one.

"Yes, a project on the Iron Age. So? What's it to you? It's not like I stole your wretched books. Anyway, I've returned them now."

"When I looked on Friday, the gap on the history shelf was still there."

"Yes, but if you haven't looked since the end of term, you won't have seen that I brought them back at the weekend."

"At the weekend? How could you have done? There's no-one on site to let you in at weekends."

He pushed his chair further back from the table and stretched out his legs.

"So? I've got the key code for the front door and the alarm code, same as Mrs Broom and Ella have for my school. We have so many joint meetings that we've always known both school's codes. It's been the Battle of Bannockburn here practically since the actual battle. Honestly, you lot ought to change your security codes more often, like we do at Hutmarton."

"Really? Just to be sure, can you remind me which books those were exactly? I'd hate to misjudge you."

I smiled sweetly, and he gave an exaggerated sigh.

"OK. Four books on the Iron Age in general, and a few thinner ones on more specialised subjects. From memory, something like *Iron-Age Man Preserved*, *People of the Wetlands*, *Lake Dwellers at Large*, *The Bog People*, and a guidebook to a Scottish tourist attraction that re-enacts the Iron Age."

"Ah yes, the Scottish Crannog Centre. It's a wonderful place, a reconstruction of an Iron Age house on stilts over Loch Tay. Do go if you ever have a chance."

My airy, upbeat tone seemed to unnerve him. He started tapping one foot in irritation.

Tommy guffawed. "The bog people? Are they people who live in toilets? Can I borrow that one, please, Sophie? I'd like to use it to gross out my little sister."

I allowed myself a small smile. "Shall I enlighten Tommy, or will you, Mr Harman? After all, you must be more expert on the topic after a whole term's study."

David Harman said nothing, staring at the kitchen as if fascinated.

"No? Then let me explain, Tommy. Bog people have been discovered in an almost perfect state of preservation in wetland environments due to the anaerobic conditions of the peat they were buried in."

Tommy frowned.

"Anaerobic means without air. It might seem an odd idea to us to bury someone in a bog, but archaeologists are very thankful that in ancient times, they did, because their practice allows us, many hundreds of years later, to learn a great deal about their societies from exhumed bodies. Exhumed means bodies people have dug up."

Tommy wrinkled his nose. "Billy wouldn't think much of that idea. When he buries people, he wants them to stay buried."

Councillor Digweed emitted a shrill cry of alarm. Kate put her mind at rest.

"Billy is our parish gravedigger. Tommy kindly helps him sometimes."

Tommy sat up straighter at Kate's acknowledgement of his important role.

"So, Mr Harman, was teaching your pupils about the bog people what gave you the idea to dump Mark Fletcher's body in Wendlebury School's septic tank?"

David Harman leapt to his feet with such force that his chair rocked.

"How dare you? Ella, who is this frightful girl? Can't you control her?"

Kate frowned. "But Sophie, I thought you just told us that the body in the tank was a woman?"

I turned to Tommy and cocked my head quizzically.

"Can you help me out here, please, Tommy?"

Tommy beamed.

"Sophie's right, Kate. It wasn't a woman. It was that missing guy in the newspaper that Billy was reading in the churchyard yesterday lunchtime. He bought a copy from the village shop after he read the one at Hector's House, because he used to know the man who went missing, and he was telling me all about him. When he was a boy, this guy used to help Billy like I do. Do you think there's a curse on people who help Billy in the graveyard? Do you think someone will try to murder me next?"

He looked to me for reassurance. When I shook my head, he continued.

"I recognised him as the missing guy straight away when I looked down the hole in the ground. The manhole, it's called. It's a good name for a hole you put a man down, isn't it? I've been watching it from my hide. Hector lent me his binoculars when I told him I'd built a hide, like he told me to."

David Harman fell back into his chair and pounded the table with his fist.

"You can say what you like, the police won't take any notice of you. You're just a kid with a crazy imagination. You're not next of kin. You've never seen him before in your life. How could you possibly have recognised him when he's covered in –"

"Mud," cut in Kate quickly.

Tommy scowled.

"Tommy may not have seen him before, but I have," I announced. "On Monday, very briefly, in the lost property cupboard, and so did Ella. Isn't that right, Ella?"

"God's honest truth," said Ella, crossing her heart with her forefinger, like children making promises in the playground.

"And what's more, I think Ian is just about to find security camera footage that will show you, Mr Harman, up to no good in the playground here on Monday."

Kate removed the cap from her fountain pen and opened her notebook to a fresh page.

"Now, David, while we're waiting for the police to arrive, why don't you take the opportunity to rehearse your side of the story?"

28 All Washed Up

"If Ella had been doing her job properly, no-one would ever have known. That cruel prig would have been out of my hair for good." David Harman was tearing his meeting papers into smaller and smaller pieces. "The septic tank was meant to be emptied last thing on Friday, after the kids had gone home, then it was to fall out of use when the school was connected to the mains drains this week. At the same time, you were going to fill the emptied septic tank with concrete, and the playground installers were going to tarmac over the sealed manhole. It's Ella's fault that it hasn't been done."

"What does that matter?" retorted Ella. "They've still got a day or two before they start resurfacing the playground. As long as the septic tank is emptied by then, it makes no difference whether it was done last Friday or today. Stop trying to score cheap points."

David Harman folded his arms. "I should have realised it was all too easy to be true."

"Easy? To kill a man?" cried Kate. "What sort of talk is that?"

David Harman shrugged. "Fletcher made it easy. After he'd moved into his temporary accommodation, he

179

accepted my invitation to come round to mine for a drink. For old times' sake, he said, before we had to 'enter into a formal professional relationship', as he put it, with him as my new boss. Him! My boss! Huh! He just couldn't stop gloating."

His voice was getting shriller with every sentence. I pitched mine low in hope of calming him.

"It must have been hard, Mr Harman, always to be beaten into second place by your old school rival."

David Harman sniffed. "What do you mean, whatever your name is?"

"Checking your old reports in the school archive, I couldn't help noticing that you and Mr Fletcher were in the same class. Every year throughout primary school, he came top of the class, and you came second, in every single subject. Most people would think that commendable. Just as they'd think being a deputy head is admirable."

With such a sullen expression, David Harman was not hard to picture as an eleven-year-old.

"Second's not first. Do you know what my mum used to say to me every last day of term when we brought home our school reports? 'The person who comes second is first loser.'" He clenched his fists on the tabletop. "All the adults thought he was so perfect. But he wasn't such a goody two-shoes as everybody thought. He could be sly and spiteful when they weren't looking. He was scared all the time that I might push him off his pedestal, so he did everything in his power to put me down. Once, he made all the kids I'd invited to my birthday party promise to stay away. And they did. Can you imagine how hurtful that was? I never dared have another birthday party. Still haven't. I couldn't bear to risk being hurt like that again."

"Wow, that's harsh," murmured Tommy.

"I wanted Mum to tell the school and get him into trouble about it, but she wouldn't. Even she used to take his side against me sometimes. And so it went on, all through big school, although thankfully at Slate Green Secondary they didn't have that stupid system with the end-of-year exams where they rank you all in the class and make your position public knowledge. I got better GCSEs and A Levels than Fletcher did, but he still got into a better university than I did, because the teachers gave him such a fabulous reference. Seeing him promoted over me to become head of Hutmarton School was a step too far. That headship is mine by rights. I've earned it. He hasn't."

Ella leaned forward. "Believe me, Mr Harman, being a head teacher is not all it's cracked up to be. Mrs Broom really needed her holiday."

David Harman glared at her.

"What do you know about responsibility? You're only a school secretary."

At Ella's sharp intake of breath, I put a restraining hand on her arm. This idiot would condemn himself irredeemably without any help from her.

"But don't you see?" David Harman continued. "I had the perfect plan. With Fletcher out of the frame, I'd be automatically made up to acting head for the start of the new school year, and the longer he was missing, the more chance I'd have to prove myself. It's the fast-track to career advancement. And then, if and when our two schools merge, having saved Hutmarton at its time of crisis, I'd almost certainly be made head of the new joint school. Especially as Mrs Broom's a woman."

Councillor Digweed shook her head in disbelief at David Harman's open bigotry. Councillor Grant raised his hand. "So what you are saying is that you, er, helped Mark Fletcher on his way?"

David Harman waved his hand.

"Obviously. If you'd read any of my applications properly, you'd remember I have a chemistry degree. It may not be a fancy MSc like Ella's –" when Ella smirked, I realised that she'd made her nuclear physics qualification up on the spur of the moment, "– but it's hardly rocket science to find a substance that would simply stop his heart. I wasn't about to disfigure him in any way or shed blood. I've just had new carpets fitted."

Councillor Grant frowned.

"So you poisoned him in your house, brought him here and dropped him in the septic tank?"

David Harman grinned. "Yes, he'd be in his very own time capsule, buried for posterity, just like the bog people my Year 4 has been studying all term."

Councillor Grant scratched his head. "How did you manage to do that without anyone noticing?"

"He didn't need to break in," I said evenly. "He could have come here any time over the weekend. He's already told us he has the key code for the front door. And if anyone hasn't remembered that, don't worry: I've been recording the whole meeting so far on my phone."

"Sunday afternoon at 4.32pm, to be precise." Ian was walking towards us across the hall, making a suitably dramatic entrance for a leading light of the Wendlebury Players. "I've just clocked him on the replay of the security video, driving down the track to the car park and pulling up beside the wheelie bins. Mark Fletcher was slumped in the front seat, looking for all the world like a sleeping passenger. But you weren't strong enough to carry his body to the manhole, were you, Mr Harman?"

182

"Of course I was," replied David Harman. "How do you think I managed to get him in my car? Asked a neighbour to give me a hand? I'm not stupid. It was even hotter on Sunday than it is today, and I wasn't going to let him exert me more than necessary. I'd planned to access the playground from the back of the school, but I couldn't, because some idiot had secured the five-bar gate with a damn great padlock. I could hardly lob him over the gate as if I were tossing a caber, and clamber over it after him. Not that I'm not strong enough –"

He gave me a smug look, as if expecting me to be impressed with his manliness.

"– that would just be silly. So when I saw the wheelie bins standing idle there, it was much easier to upend him into one of them, trundle him round to the front of the school and in through the front door."

He paused to slurp coffee from his cup.

"Then you let yourself in," I went on, watching brown drips spatter his pale shirt.

"I saw on the security camera footage that you brought something else with you in a carrier bag," put in Ian. "And that was?"

"My library books, of course. I was returning my library books."

"Like that's a redeeming feature," muttered Ella.

"So I let myself in using the key code, and wheeled him across to the French doors, the only other access to the playground when the five-bar gate is closed."

Kate sighed. "We really need to start using less well-known entry codes, Ella."

"At least this one's better than the one it replaced, 1066," replied Ella.

"The War of Jenkins' Ear would be better," put in Mr Barnard, suddenly turning interesting. "Although you'd have to use eight digits as it lasted nine years: 1739–1748."

David Harman glared at all three of them in turn, as if trying to intimidate chattering children in the classroom.

"Anyway, I couldn't get the damn things to open. I hadn't realised there'd be a separate code; I assumed it would be the same as the front door. So I had no choice but to stash him somewhere until Monday, when the doors would doubtless be propped open against the heat. Then I'd be able to pick my moment to sneak in and move him to his final resting place."

"But why the lost property cupboard?" asked Ella.

He waved his hand dismissively. "I couldn't risk leaving him in the bin as I didn't know which day your bin men come in Wendlebury. If they came on Monday, my secret would have been out. Besides, nobody ever rushes to clear the lost property cupboard during the holidays, not once the parents have taken all the good stuff on the last day of term."

"Actually, I do," said Ella. "It's always one of my first jobs of the holidays. For health and safety in case any perishables have been left in there."

"Quite right too." Councillor Digweed nodded approval.

"Really?" He raised his eyebrows. "We never do at Hutmarton. But that was the easy bit. I thought I'd be able to creep in round the back way, via the open gate, on the Monday morning when Ella and Ian were otherwise occupied and make the transfer then."

"Make the transfer?" Kate queried.

"Slip him into the septic tank when no-one was looking. I admit I hadn't reckoned on the playground workmen being here already when they've got all summer to install the new equipment. But when I saw their van in the school car park on the Monday morning, I watched them work for a bit to see how they were operating. I soon realised that every so often, they'd go down the bottom of the field for a cigarette, like naughty kids. So all I had to do was wait till they'd all downed tools, sneak in through the French doors, which were propped open, as I'd anticipated, and do a quick dash from the cupboard to the manhole cover with the body over my shoulder."

"But you can't have done," cried Ella. "Ian and I were here. We'd have noticed you."

"Ha! Not you! You were busy gossiping with your tea lady in your office. I could hear you through the door." He turned to Kate. "How can Wendlebury afford a tea lady on its budget, by the way? I want a tea lady for Hutmarton. Anyway, Ian was stuck into cleaning the boys' toilets, helpfully singing 'My Favourite Things' at the top his voice so that I knew exactly where he was. It was the work of moments to sneak Fletcher out. Splish, splash, splosh, job done. I was on my way home before those layabouts working on the playground had even finished their smoke."

"So the workmen didn't see a thing either?" asked Kate.

"Nope. They kept their backs turned, so that no-one up at the school would see them smoking. To be on the safe side, I'd slipped on one of Ian's brown duster coats that he'd left lying on the picnic table outside, so if they did see me from a distance, they'd think I was Ian. We're alike in build and colouring, even if he is twice my age."

"So that's where my spare coat went!" cried Ian. "Not that I'd have wanted it back after that, thank you very much."

"Caretaker, you should take more care." Ian went rigid at hearing Mrs Broom's mantra from David Harman's lips. "Of course, I had planned for the eventuality of being seen by either Ian or Ella. I'd left the library books I was returning in the lost property cupboard at the same time I dumped Fletcher's body there. If I heard Ian or Ella coming while I was in the entrance hall, I could just grab the books and say I'd dropped by to return them.

"As I was cycling back to Hutmarton – oh yes, on Monday I came on my bike so as not to make myself conspicuous parking my car – I was a little startled to be overtaken by Ian driving past with Ella in the passenger seat."

He turned to Kate again.

"Are these two carrying on or something? I know Ella plays the field, but isn't the caretaker old enough to be her grandad?"

"How dare you!" cried Ella. "No offence, Ian, by the way."

Ian's smile suggested he'd taken David Harman's accusation as a compliment.

I explained on Ella's behalf.

"Ian was taking Ella home because she'd fainted after seeing something nasty in the lost property cupboard. As had I, before it mysteriously disappeared. Or not so mysteriously, as it turns out. And I'm not the tea lady. I'm the school librarian."

For the first time, David Harman looked taken aback. "Really? Good thing I brought my books back, then."

"They were still in the lost property cupboard when I was clearing it out on my return," said Ian. "And I gave them to Sophie to put back in the library."

David Harman rubbed his hands together. "So, all's well that ends well."

"Jolly good," said Mr Barnard, reverting to type.

For a moment, the only sound in the room was the scratching of Kate's fountain pen. Then she stopped writing.

"But David, it's awful enough that you murdered poor Mark Fletcher, but what on earth possessed you to bring him here to dispose of him? Far be it from me to put ideas into your head, in which, goodness knows, there's already too much going on, but weren't there less complicated ways to do it?"

Like laying a new patio, I was thinking.

David Harman sat back in his chair, stretched out his legs, and put his hands behind his head. Was it a relief to have it all out in the open at last? Surely he had never believed he was going to get away with it? He looked as if he was enjoying being the centre of attention, interpreting our horrified reactions as adulation at his brilliance.

"But don't you see? Here's where it all began. Fletcher had been so happy here, lording it over me all through primary school. It would be poetic justice for him to be shut away in the sealed pit, preserved below the school playground where no-one would ever find him."

"As innocent children played above his head," murmured Councillor Digweed, pale as milk. I got up to refill her coffee cup, and she took a grateful swig.

I glanced at the wall clock above the serving hatch.

"Just before the police arrive, Mr Harman, I've one last question. About those notes you sent to me and Hector. Were they meant to frighten us into silence? I can understand why you might wish to intimidate me, if you thought I'd seen the body in the lost property cupboard, but why Hector? He didn't come up to the school until after the body had disappeared, and he didn't even believe it existed. In a horrible way, it was like he was on your side, trying to convince Ella and me that we'd been seeing things. So why intimidate him, too?"

But David Harman didn't linger long enough to answer. Spotting the police marching across the hall towards us, he dashed out through the French doors and sprinted over the playground towards the open side gate and the fields beyond.

29 Gated

"Who would believe that old playground rivalries could warp a person's judgement into adulthood?" Kate raked her fingers through her hair. "Especially someone who's spent their career in teaching. It never does any good to keep comparing yourself to others. No matter how bright or capable or athletic you are, there'll always be someone smarter or slicker or faster."

Having caught up with David Harman in the field behind the school, the police had led him away, and the forensics team was due to arrive shortly to examine the scene of the crime, including the septic tank – poor souls. Then a police ambulance would remove the body.

Councillor Grant coughed. "Assessing progress each year is all very well, but telling the children and their parents every child's rank in the class was always a terrible idea. Even so, I never thought it would lead to murder. I know people complain about the current system, but it's all relative. Still, if you will excuse me, I think Councillor Digweed and I should head off now. We'll lose more time tomorrow making our statement at the police station, and we're already behind where we should be at the start of the holidays."

"Mr Barnard, please may I have a private word with you before you go?" said Kate, gathering her papers into her leather folio. "Tommy, you run along now, and Ella and Sophie, I suggest you take the rest of the day off. But Ella, if you have any concerns or need me to help you through this awful business, do call me, any time, day or night. That's what we governors are here for."

I hoped her fellow governors shared her generous attitude.

Ella and I returned to her office, where we slumped down in the chairs at her meeting table. She looked as drained as I felt.

"I was worried it was Ian, you know," said Ella, all of a sudden. "That's why I didn't want him to drive me home. I thought he had murdered someone, and that he was just pretending not to see the body."

I didn't like to mention that at one point I'd wondered whether she and he were in league. I felt awful about that now.

"Ian's very convincing when he plays the baddie in the Wendlebury Players' productions," I replied, trying to make her feel better.

"I heard that, Sophie," came Ian's voice at the door. "Thank you very much. That's the nicest thing you've ever said about me. Although you're forgetting you cast me as Joseph in your nativity play last Christmas."

I grinned. "That was much more like typecasting."

Just then, the front doorbell sounded, and we all looked at each other, wondering who on earth it could be now. Ian, being nearest, went to open it, admitting Hector, who breezed into Ella's office, hands in the pockets of his jeans.

"Hello, is this a private party, or can anyone join in?"

190

I leapt up and threw my arms around him, even though it was still opening hours. The tension of the afternoon was catching up with me.

"Is that a yes or a no?" I heard him ask above my sobs. "I was starting to get worried as to why you were taking so long to deliver a box of cakes, then I saw a police car go past, then a police van, heading in your direction. So I left Billy in charge of the shop and popped up to make sure you were all OK."

Before we had time to bring him up to date, Kate came striding in, wearing her determined look. It's never far away.

"Come along, girls, I told you to go home," she declared. "Get away from the premises and distract yourselves. Take yourselves off to Cirencester or Nailsworth or somewhere like that." She glanced at my frock. "Go clothes shopping or get your nails done. Treat yourselves."

"What about seeing the forensics team in?" asked Ella. "And locking up? I don't think Mrs Broom would be very happy if I bunked off for half the afternoon."

Kate held up her hands to quell her protest. "Ian can take care of all that, can't you, Ian? You're much more than a caretaker." Ian's chest swelled with pride. "And may I suggest that before you finish tonight, you change the front door code, even if it is shutting the door after this particular horse has bolted. Besides, Ella, Mrs Broom is currently sunning herself in the south of France and we'll let her get on with it until her return. When she does find out what's transpired, your taking a few hours off will be the least of her worries."

Hector stared open-mouthed from Kate to Ella to Ian to me.

"Transpired? What's transpired? Why is a forensics team on its way? What have I missed?"

Kate went behind the desk and put her hands lightly on Ella's shoulders, raising her up from her chair like a levitationist, before pointing her towards the door. I let go of Hector.

"Actually, I think an afternoon off sounds a very good idea. Kate, can you please fill Hector in on the details? I don't think I can bear to go over it again just yet. Come on, Ella. Let's go. I can't remember the last time I went clothes shopping."

That clinched it for Ella. Pausing only to pick up her bag and her keys, she grabbed my arm and dragged me out behind her.

30 The Nun's Secret

As Ella and I drove back into the village in the early evening, the Reverend Murray and Tommy were standing outside the vicarage, deep in conversation.

"Can you drop me off here, please, Ella? I want to make sure Tommy's OK. I feel a bit bad about how I used him this afternoon. I hope he's not traumatised by the experience. From his hide at the edge of the field, he must have seen far more than is good for an impressionable teenager."

Ella braked and pulled over to the side of the road.

"Tommy must be feeling low if he's turned to the vicar for counselling," she remarked. "Either that or he's broadcasting his version of today's events around the village, contrary to the instructions of the police. We don't want him scaring parents and children off from returning to school in September. I'm terrified that all our kids will transfer to Hutmarton School, even though it has neither head nor deputy now. It could spell the end for Wendlebury Primary, you know."

"What parent would send their child to a school where the deputy head murdered the head teacher? I hardly think you need worry, Ella."

She wrinkled her nose.

"I'll come and have a word with him anyway."

As we got out of the car, we were surprised to discover that the topic of their conversation was not murder, but spelling.

"Tommy, it's definitely spelt with an 'o', not a 'u'," the vicar was saying. "It's an abbreviation. A short form."

Tommy's brow creased. "You mean I've been spelling it wrong all this time?"

"And pronouncing it wrong, I'm afraid."

"No, I'm saying it right. It's like the none in none-toxic, isn't it?"

The vicar sighed. "The word is non-toxic, from the Greek: *toxikon pharmakon*, meaning poison for arrows, prefix *non* from Middle English. Non has a short o." Seeing us approach, he shook his head at Ella. "Ms Berry, I've a suggestion for your teacher in charge of English. Teach your children the difference between the prefix non and the word none. And, indeed, nun."

"Nun, as in the opposite of monk," added Tommy, ever helpful.

The vicar was clutching a small piece of paper that looked familiar. It bore the same distinctive handwriting of the threatening letters that Hector and I had received.

"Since when have you developed an interest in monks and nuns, Tommy?" I asked him.

"I haven't. The vicar's just got all confused. What I mean is that person who doesn't want you to know his real name. You know."

When he gave me a stagey wink, I feared he was referring to the pseudonym under which Hector wrote his romantic novels. The only people who were meant to know about that besides me and Hector were his parents and his brother.

194

"He means anonymous," sighed the vicar. "When I was a lad, we used to sign things 'A Nony Mouse', thinking we were the height of wit, though goodness knows what we thought Nony meant. A word fit for Lewis Carroll's 'Jabberwocky', perhaps." He held out the slip of paper for me to see. I read it aloud.

"To the Vicker. You are making a grave mistake. Correct the error of your ways. From A Nun."

I gasped. "Good heavens, whatever have you been up to, Vicar?"

The vicar tapped the letter.

"To add insult to injury, he wants me to give him 50p for delivering his misspelt missive to me. Mind you, to be fair to the lad –"

"I think you should be," put in Tommy.

"– he's right about the grave mistake. Someone has mixed up the wooden crosses on the two most recent graves. You know, those little temporary markers bearing the names of the deceased, which identify the occupant of a newly dug plot until the ground has settled enough to withstand the permanent headstone. To show the wrong name on a plot is a terrible thing to happen – most upsetting to the bereaved. I must have words with old Billy."

He paused.

"Actually, Tommy, despite your poor spelling, your message is worth 50p of any clergyman's money." He slipped his hand into his trouser pocket, jingling his change as he felt for the straight edges of a 50p piece. "Here you go, my boy. Although I'm not entirely sure why you didn't just tell me, or indeed swap the crosses back to their rightful places without more ado."

Tommy smiled at the coin in his palm.

"Don't worry, I swapped them back as soon as I knew. So don't you go swapping them again, Vicar. But you're right, it's been a lot of work, even for 50p a time, what with writing the letters and delivering them. I'm not sure I can keep it up all through the holidays. It won't leave me time for anything else."

"Hang on a minute, Tommy," I said. "Do you mean you wrote the vicar's letter? And mine? And Hector's? Are you the, er, nun?"

Tommy shrugged.

"Actually, I prefer the vicar's Nony Mouse. I wish my name was Nony."

"But why on earth did you write those letters?"

"Why not? Didn't you like them?" Tommy huffed. "I don't know, I get no thanks for trying to encourage people. I'd have thought your message was clear enough. You went on that writing holiday to learn how to write books. Your old auntie was good at writing books. I just wanted to tell you I think you'll be as good at it as she was one day. So that's what I put: what happened to your auntie will happen to you. Isn't that a cheery message to receive?"

I exhaled loudly. "Oh, I see what you mean now. And what about Hector's message?"

"I'm not sure if I should say it out loud, Sophie. Come here and I'll whisper it to you."

We stepped aside so he could whisper in my ear. Then he stood back and fixed me with a quizzical look.

"I hope I haven't spoiled the surprise? You did know about it, didn't you?" He'd whispered, "Hermy One Minty."

I laughed aloud. All that hooch gone down the drain for nothing! I wondered how Tommy had found out about Hector's pseudonym and alter ego, the romantic novelist Hermione Minty.

"No, Tommy, I've known about that for ages. But I think the sooner you find a different use for that post box, the better."

Tommy looked relieved. "OK, I'll give it some thought."

And with that, he strode off down the High Street towards the shop, chucking his 50p from hand to hand.

My smile faded as Ella began to tell the vicar about the body in the septic tank. As he was also a school governor, he needed to know.

"Thank you, Ella," he said, gently, "but don't worry. Kate called in at the vicarage a little while ago to tell me the tragic tale. We'll be working closely with the council and the police to keep it confidential for the sake of the school's reputation and the mental health of all concerned. And Mrs Broom, too, when she returns from her well-earned holiday."

"I have to say, I'll be glad to have her back," said Ella. "I'm beginning to have a new appreciation of Mrs Broom. Just think, if David Harman had got away with his dreadful plan, and our schools had merged at Hutmarton, I might have ended up with him as my boss."

The vicar gave her shoulder a reassuring pat.

"I think it's more likely they'll consolidate the two schools at Wendlebury, with neither a head nor a deputy in place at Hutmarton now. Bear in mind that not all crimes have to be emblazoned across the papers or plastered all over social media. In the meantime, it's a beautiful evening, so I suggest you make the most of it before the heatwave breaks. I hear a summer storm is on its way."

31 New Beginnings

Hector spread the sky-blue rug on the grassy knoll while I opened the picnic basket and took out some plates.

"Not such impressive contents this time, I'm afraid, as this was a bit impromptu."

I took ham sandwiches, chocolate butterfly cakes and strawberry tarts out of their plastic bags and decanted them onto the plates.

"Doesn't matter. It's just nice to be away from the village for a bit."

"And there's you all poshed up, too." He eyed the new forget-me-not blue linen sundress that Ella had helped me choose that afternoon in Cirencester. "That dress brings out the colour of your eyes. Not like those murky Indian prints you've been wearing lately."

I wrinkled my nose.

"Actually, I was thinking of passing those on to Carol, if she'd like them. She's wilting in those old nylon dresses of her mum's." I spread the full skirt that flared out from the fitted bodice, feeling like Alice in Wonderland. "I liked the shape so much that I bought a dove-grey one in the same style."

Hector nodded his approval. "Good, I'm glad. It's nice to see you smiling again, too, in spite of – well, you know. I'm very impressed. Kate told me you solved the mystery of the body in the lost property cupboard singlehandedly. Wrong-footing David Harman by saying the victim was a woman was genius. I'm sorry I doubted you at the start of the week."

I helped myself to a ham sandwich.

"That's OK. Ian and Ella helped too. I didn't quite believe it myself half the time, nor did I want to."

Hector shook his head sadly. "And all because of schoolboy jealousy. What a pointless waste of two talented men."

"Yes, jealousy is so destructive." I resolved to be especially nice to Anastasia at work the next day. "Anyway, Ella said to me a few days ago that you and I spend too much time in each other's pockets. It's been a timely way to prove my independence."

Hector twisted the wire casing off the top of a bottle of sparkling wine, then gripped the cork and turned the bottle. I held two tumblers up for him to fill.

"No problem. When you didn't come back, I got Billy to man the trade counter and Anastasia to run the tearoom so that I could go up to the school to check everything was OK."

I held up my glass against the sunshine, watching the bubbles rising to the surface and bursting.

"So I'm dispensable now, am I?"

He gave a wry smile. "Actually, seeing Anastasia in action in the tearoom made me realise what a brilliant job you do there. I confess I haven't given you enough credit for how much you've grown the tearoom business and made it your own, as well as boosting the bookshop's profits, what with your reading lessons for children and special events and activities to keep the punters coming in. More importantly, you don't make fun of the boss when you think he's not listening."

"What do you mean?"

He took a sip of his wine. "Just before I called Anastasia downstairs this afternoon, I heard her over the baby monitor talking to her boyfriend on her mobile phone. She told him she thinks I'm about fifty and that I curl and dye my hair. Then she did an uncanny impression of me being nice to customers."

I put my hand over my mouth to hide my smile.

"Don't worry, Hector, when you're eighteen, everyone over twenty-five looks ancient. So are you going to sack her for insubordination?"

It was Hector's turn to laugh. "No, I thought I'd keep her on until the end of September so we can have that holiday in Scotland you keep talking about. But I've made it clear that after that, it'll be just the two of us. Unless spending all this time at the school lately has made you hanker after going back into teaching? Or to retrain as a librarian?"

"Ha! This week's experience has hardly been the best advert for working in a school." Then a terrible thought struck me. "Why, you're not thinking of closing the shop down, are you? You're not giving it up to write full time?"

When I'd flown out to Greece, I'd been wondering whether Hector was too staid, having no higher ambition than to run a bookshop for the rest of his life, but lately I had started to understand why.

"Good lord, no, I couldn't do that to the village. Rural house prices diminish with the loss of every local shop, and the villagers would miss the tearoom, too, and the extra coaching you offer to the children. And they'd miss you. Hector's House is so much more than just a bookshop, don't you think?"

I had to agree. "Especially now you're diversifying even further."

He moved the plate of sandwiches that was between us on the rug so that he could put his arm around me.

"Actually, the best bit of diversification I've ever done was to bring you into the mix."

I put both my arms around him and rested my head on his shoulder.

"That's a lovely thing to say." I wanted to bask in the moment, but at the same time, I was eager to enthuse him about our Scottish holiday. "You can make it a bit of a working holiday if you like, Hector. We can have such fun hunting for more stock for your Curiosities Shop in Scotland. There are loads of charity shops where you can pick up all sorts of collectible books you'd not find south of the border. Plus you'll be able to deliver to my mum in person that Gaelic book with the intriguing inscription that you found at the car boot sale in Clevedon back in January."

"Diversifying's fine up to a point, but I confess Tommy's note was a bit of a wake-up call. Honestly, that boy, you never know what he's going to do next."

At that point, there was a rush of air above our heads and a large butterfly net landed neatly over one of the cakes. At the other end of the stick was Tommy, still in his camouflage gear.

"You have to be stealthy with butterflies," he was saying as he bent to pick up his prey. "Or rather, butterfly cakes." He beamed. "Butterfly cakes, geddit? Can I have this one, by the way? I'm hungry. My new hobby's quite tiring."

"Go on, then, Tommy," said Hector. "I'm not sure either of us would fancy it after it's been inside your butterfly net. Where did you get that net from, anyway?"

Tommy swung the stick over his shoulder, nearly poking me in the eye.

"I swapped it with the vicar for my post box. He said he'd been wanting a box like that to use for suggestions in church. He's given me a book about butterflies, too. He said butterflies were his favourite hobby when he was my age, because he grew up in the olden days when they didn't have the internet or mobile phones. But he said not to keep any I catch, just to look at them and let them fly away again. I wouldn't want to murder butterflies, anyway.

"I hope you won't mind if I don't stay for the rest of your picnic. The vicar said it's going to rain in a little while, and I don't think butterflies go out in the rain, so I'm going home to read my book instead, then I'll know what to look for tomorrow."

He pointed his net towards the horizon, where the distant hills lay mauve and misty. "Did you see that flash of lightning? Look, and another one. Wow! That was a good one!"

As Hector shaded his eyes against the still bright sunlight, a rumble of thunder echoed among the dark clouds rolling towards us across the valley. He laid a hand gently on my knee.

"Perhaps we'd better finish our picnic back at my flat, eh, Sophie?"

As we gathered everything into the basket, fat drops of rain began to dapple the pale linen of my new dress. Tommy watched us pack, talking non-stop.

"Still, I don't care if it does rain, because it won't spoil the summer holidays. You know, I was wrong about the school holidays, because so far it hasn't been boring at all. It's been brilliant. Hector, do you want to come and see the hide I've built on the school playing field, like you said? If you can spot it, that is. I got in there through a hole in the hedge that no-one else knows about. Those workmen building the new playground didn't know about it, anyway. They're really nice and they've said I can do some digging for them if I like, and you know how good I am at digging. Billy always says I'm good at digging."

Anxious to beat the encroaching storm, I rolled up the sky-blue rug and tucked it inside the basket. Hector got to his feet and reached down to haul me up. Tommy, with his free hand, picked up the basket, happy to help by carrying it for us.

As the three of us wandered back up the Cotswold Way towards the village, the thunder rumbled softly at our backs.

If you enjoyed reading this book,
you might like to spread the word to other readers
by leaving a brief review online –
or just tell your friends!
Thank you.

Like to know when Debbie Young's
next book is ready for you to read?
Sign up for her free Readers' Club via her website
and you'll also receive a free download
of the e-book *The Pride of Peacocks*,
available exclusively to Readers' Club members.

www.authordebbieyoung.com

You may like to connect with Debbie Young
via social media:

Facebook @authordebbieyoung
Twitter @DebbieYoungBN
Instagram @debbieyoungauthor

Acknowledgements

Enormous thanks to all the people who have helped make this a better book:

- Orna Ross, as ever, for her wise and sensitive mentoring of the creative process (google her *Go Creative!* Series)
- Lucienne Boyce, for her valuable guidance and sound judgement on the story and the details
- Alison Jack, my patient, capable, dependable editor
- Rachel Lawston of Lawston Design for another wonderful book cover
- Dan Gooding of Zedolus for proofreading
- Poet Liezel Graham for identifying the title of the HG Wells story that Hector refers to, *The Presence by the Fire*, which I first read long ago and had been searching for ever since
- Juliette Lawson, author of *A Borrowed Past*, for technical advice on primary school education

Any mistakes remaining are my own.
Debbie Young

Best Murder in Show
(Sophie Sayers Village Mysteries #1)

A dead body on a carnival float at the village show.

A clear case of murder in plain sight, thinks new arrival Sophie Sayers – but why do none of the villagers agree? What dark secrets are they hiding to prevent her unmasking the murderer, and who holds the key to the mystery?

Can Sophie unearth the clues tucked away in this outwardly idyllic Cotswold village before anyone else comes to harm, not least herself?

For fans of cosy mysteries everywhere, Best Murder in Show will make you laugh out loud at the idiosyncrasies of English country life and rack your brains to discover the murderer before Sophie can.

"A cracking example of cosy crime"
Katie Fforde

Available in paperback, ebook and audio
ISBN 978-1-911223-13-9 (paperback)

Trick or Murder?
(Sophie Sayers Village Mysteries #2)

Just when Sophie Sayers is starting to feel at home in the Cotswold village of Wendlebury Barrow, a fierce new vicar arrives, quickly offending her and everyone else he meets.

Banning the villagers' Halloween celebrations seems the last straw, even though he instead revives the old English Guy Fawkes' tradition. What dark secret is he hiding about Sophie's boss, the beguiling bookseller Hector Munro? And whose body is that outside the village bookshop? Not to mention the one buried beneath the vicar's bonfire piled high with sinister effigies.

Sophie's second adventure will have you laughing out loud as you try to solve the mystery, in the company of engaging new characters as well as familiar favourites from Best Murder in Show.

> *"Debbie Young delves into the awkwardness*
> *of human nature in a deft and funny way:*
> *Miss Marple meets Bridget Jones."*
> *Belinda Pollard, Wild Crimes series*

Available in paperback and ebook
ISBN 978-1-911223-20-7 (paperback)

Murder in the Manger
(Sophie Sayers Village Mysteries #3)

When Sophie Sayers's plans for a cosy English country Christmas are interrupted by the arrival of her ex-boyfriend, Damian, her troubles are only just beginning. Before long, the whole village stands accused of murder.

Damian says he's come to direct the village nativity play, but Sophie thinks he's up to no good. What are those noises coming from his van? Who is the stranger lurking in the shadows? And whose baby, abandoned in the manger, disappears in plain sight?

Enjoy the fun of a traditional Christmas festive season with echoes of Charles Dickens' A Christmas Carol *as Sophie seeks a happy ending for her latest village mystery – and her budding romance with charming local bookseller Hector Munro.*

"The funniest opening line in a novel, period.
I can't get enough of the Sophie Sayers Village Mystery series."
Wendy H Jones,
author of DI Shona McKenzie thrillers

Available in paperback and ebook
ISBN 978-1-911223-22-1 (paperback)

Murder by the Book
(Sophie Sayers Village Mysteries #4)

Sophie Sayers's plans for a romantic Valentine's night at the village pub didn't include someone being shoved to their death down its ancient well.

But as no-one witnessed the crime, will it ever be solved in this close-knit English village where everyone knows each other – and half of them are also related?

It will be if Sophie Sayers has anything to do with it. But can she stop eager teenage sidekick Tommy Crowe unmasking her boyfriend Hector's secret identity in the process, causing chaos to his precarious bookshop business?

A whole shoal of red herrings will keep you guessing as tempers flare and old feuds catch fire in this lively mystery about love, loyalty and family ties, set in the heart of the idyllic English Cotswolds. Idyllic unless you happen to be a murder victim.

"An assured and delicious sequel."
Susan Grossey, author of the Sam Plank Mysteries

Available in paperback and ebook
ISBN 978-1-911223-26-9 (paperback)

Springtime for Murder
(Sophie Sayers Village Mysteries #5)

When Bunny Carter, the old lady from the Manor House, is discovered in an open grave, Sophie Sayers is sure it's a case of foul play. But when it comes to suspects, she's spoiled for choice.

One of Bunny's squabbling children from three different husbands? Petunia Lot from the Cats Prevention charity, always angling for a legacy?

All these and more had motive and opportunity.

But which is to blame? And can Sophie and her boyfriend, village bookseller Hector Munro, stop them before they strike again?

A lively array of eccentrics joins the regular cast in this compelling story of family, friendship, love and loss.

While the story includes plenty of Debbie Young's renowned wit and British humour, it's also thoughtful and poignant, reflecting Sophie's growing wisdom, self-reliance and skill as self-appointed amateur village sleuth.

"The latest dose of Sophie Sayers slips down perfectly."
Susan Grossey, author of the Sam Plank Mysteries

Available in paperback and ebook
ISBN 978-1911223344 (paperback)

Murder Your Darlings
(Sophie Sayers Village Mysteries #6)

When Sophie Sayers joins a writers' retreat on a secluded Greek island, she's hoping to find inspiration and perhaps a little adventure. Away from her rural English comfort zone, she also takes stock of her relationship with her boyfriend Hector.

But scarcely has the writing course begun when bestselling romantic novelist Marina Milanese disappears on a solo excursion to an old windmill. First on the scene, Sophie is prime suspect for Marina's murder. When a storm prevents the Greek police from landing on the island to investigate, Sophie must try to solve the crime herself – not easy, when everyone at the retreat has a motive.

As she strives to uncover the truth about Marina's fate, Sophie arrives at a life-changing decision about her own future.

Shortlisted for The 2021 Selfies Award,
given to the best self-published adult fiction in the UK

Available in paperback and ebook
ISBN 978-1911223559 (paperback)

First in a New Series:

SECRETS AT ST BRIDE'S
(St Bride's School Stories #1)

When Gemma Lamb takes a job at a quirky English girls' boarding school, she believes she's found the perfect escape route from her controlling boyfriend – until she discovers the rest of the staff are hiding sinister secrets…

Meet Hairnet, the eccentric headmistress who doesn't hold with academic qualifications; Oriana Bliss, Head of Maths and master of disguise; Joscelyn Spryke, the suspiciously rugged Head of PE; Geography teacher Mavis Brook, surreptitiously selling off library books; creepy night watchman Max Security, with his network of hidden tunnels. Even McPhee, the school cat, is leading a double life.

Tucked away in the school's beautiful private estate in the Cotswolds, can Gemma stay safe and build an independent future? With a little help from her new friends, including some worldly-wise pupils, she's going to give it her best shot.

Perfect for anyone who grew up hooked on Chalet School, Malory Towers, St Clare's and other classic school stories, this series is set in the same world as the Sophie Sayers Village Mysteries series and includes a little crossover.

"The perfect book."
Katie Fforde

Available in paperback and ebook
ISBN 978-1911223436 (paperback)